GW01085998

The

John Rowe Townsend
The Runaways

Adapted by
David Fickling

Oxford University Press

Oxford University Press, Walton Street, Oxford OX2 6DP

Oxford London Glasgow New York Toronto
Melbourne Wellington Kuala Lumpur Singapore
Hong Kong Tokyo Delhi Bombay Calcutta Madras
Karachi Nairobi Dar es Salaam Cape Town

First published 1979
Reprinted 1980

The Runaways
1000 headword level

Set, printed and bound in Great Britain by
Cox & Wyman Ltd, Reading
Typeset in Intertype Garamond

I

... He was walking on cliffs, somewhere on the South Coast. Somewhere quiet and beautiful. White chalky cliffs where the green hills came to a stop. It was a clear blue day. He could hear sea-birds calling. There was nobody in sight. The cry for help came from far below. He stepped to the edge and looked down. She was lying completely still. She was hurt. ...

'Now, you must eat good meals,' said his mother.

'Yes.'

'And don't stay indoors all day. Go for walks.'

'Yes.'

'And put plenty of clothes on if you go out in the evenings. It's September and the nights are getting cold.'

'Yes.'

'And don't let any strangers into the house.'

'Yes. I mean no.'

'You're not listening. You never listen.'

'I am listening.'

The boy was tall, very tall, and thin. The boy was almost seventeen. He was fair-haired and wore glasses. The boy's name was Graham Hollis. He lived with his parents in a town called Crimley. The boy was day-dreaming.

... He was walking on cliffs, somewhere on the South Coast. Somewhere quiet and beautiful. The cry for help came from far below. She was lying completely still. She must be hurt. He didn't stop to think. He climbed over the edge of the cliff. He was there beside her. Her eyes were green, and her hair was long and dark.

'Oh, thank you,' she breathed. He put his arm around her ... gently. ...

'I still think he should come to Ireland with us,' his mother said to his father.

'You know I'm always car sick,' said Graham.

'You're never car sick if you want to go somewhere.'

'It's too late now,' said Mr Hollis. 'I'll go and get the suitcases.'

... 'Are you hurt?' Graham asked the girl.

'It's my leg,' she breathed. 'I think it's better now. . . .'

'You're just being difficult. Uncle Roger and Aunt Josie love seeing you at Pool-on-Sea. You don't have to stay here alone. It isn't natural at your age.'

'It'll be quiet. I can study.'

'Well, don't work *too* hard.'

'I need to pass the exam next June. Dad is always telling me.'

'I know,' said Mrs Hollis, 'but you're only sixteen. Other boys of your age are out enjoying life. Well, I suppose you don't go to wild parties. I don't have to worry about *that*. I hear about such things, but it's hard to believe them. Try to be grown-up and don't do anything silly.'

'One minute you want me to enjoy myself,' said Graham. 'Next minute I'm having wild parties all over the house. Make up your mind.'

'I'm not happy about leaving you. That's the long and the short of it,' Mrs Hollis said.

'Come on now!' Mr Hollis called from the doorway. 'Graham, you can put the two big suitcases in the car.'

Graham walked out with a suitcase in each hand. In the wide Victorian avenue the trees were yellow. The leaves were starting to fall. Mrs Hollis came down the drive, carrying her bag.

'Make sure the doors are locked at night. And close the downstairs windows.'

'Yes,' said Graham. 'Yes, Mother. Yes. Yes.'

'And don't eat fried food all the time! It isn't good for you.'

'And remember to write to us.'

'Yes.'

Mr and Mrs Hollis got into the car. The car drove off. Twenty yards along the street it stopped. His mother put her head out of the window.

'Don't forget to change your underclothes,' she called.

—They're gone. Peace at last. The street's empty now. It's a fine autumn day. The sun's coming through, just over the roof-tops.

—Go back into the house. Silent, still. You can hear your own foot-steps, and the clock. Feel sad for a moment. A week without parents. Long quiet hours of freedom to do as you wish.

—Perhaps you could ask John Wyatt round? Talk Photography or cook a meal together. You could, but you don't have to. It's nice to be a little lonely, even a little bored. Who wants to see John Wyatt anyway?

. . . He pulled her to safety at the top of the cliff. She lay in the sunshine, her head resting on his jacket.

'I'll go for help,' he told her. But she put out a hand to touch his.

'Not just yet,' she said. 'Don't leave me . . .'

—Now then, Graham! Come on boy. No more of that rub-bish.

—Nothing wrong with it.

—Nothing right with it either! Dreaming. You ought to write a book about it. *How to Waste Time* by Graham Hollis.

—All right, all right, we know what it's all about. We know what's missing in your life. We know what you need. You'll have to go where all the young people go. Where Ken Harper goes and John Wyatt and Beth Edwards.

Go to that awful disco, where you'll find 'The Crimley Girl', Beth Edwards. Out every night in Crimley. The centre of the world and twenty years behind the times!

You can keep Beth Edwards. And all like her.

. . . Her eyes were bright and her hair was long and dark. She wasn't like any girl in Crimley. She was running in front of him, calling 'You can't catch me.' Running down on to the sands and into the sea. . . .

—Come off it, boy. Write out five hundred times, 'I must not save dream girls in danger. I must not save dream girls. I must not save. I must not. I must. I.'

7

—Go for a walk, mother said. Yes, it's a good idea. A walk will get you out of the house. Put your shoes on and lock all the doors. Don't forget your keys! Set off up the hill.

—Half-way up the hill already. You can see nearly the whole town from here. Sit down, boy, take a look. Not for the first time. Crimley.

—You're here for life, boy.

—God help me.

—God won't! It's all planned. Pass the exam next year and go into Father's office. Pass more exams, and then – 'Hollis & Son, Accountants.' 'And *Son*.' That's you. From the day Dad began.

'Hollis & Son.' Small town accountants. Accountants never move. A lifetime spent in Crimley. What's wrong with Crimley? Everything's wrong with Crimley!

—Crimley dead-and-alive. Crimley: one cinema, one Bingo hall, a few clubs and nothing to do on Sundays.

—You've seen enough of it for now. Get on with that walk.

... And so the days passed in the South Coast village. They swam each morning and sometimes went sailing. Or they might take an evening walk on the cliffs where they met. Her name was – what was her name? Her name was Barbara. It had to end, of course. He kissed her gently on the lips for the first and last time. ...

—Come on, Graham! Don't get carried away. Forget her. She's only a dream. Get back to real life. Down the hill and home.

It seems years since they left. It's only twelve hours. Silence is good but a little sad. It feels strange to watch television by yourself. During the summer all the shows are repeats. Dead loss! I might phone John Wyatt.

'Hullo, Mrs Wyatt? Is John in? Oh, I see. Yes, of course, Saturday night. Yes, everybody is out on a Saturday night. Yes, tell him I rang. Tell him it was Graham. Graham Hollis. Hollis. Thank you, Mrs Wyatt. Goodbye.'

Everyone is out on a Saturday night. Everyone but me. You're nearly seventeen, Graham, and you can't stay at home for ever.

—Anyway, there's plenty of school work to do.

—Oh, to hell with school work.

—I must go out. I think I'll take a walk along the High Street. Where the bright lights and the fun are. What bright lights and what fun?

—Put your coat on. It's starting to get cold in the evenings. Remember what Mother said? Do you have to do what Mother says?

—Along to the corner and down the hill into Crimley High Street. Past the furniture store, past Woolworths, past Marks & Spencers. Plenty of people still around. Boys and girls, arm in arm.

. . . Perhaps he hadn't seen the last of her after all. She might visit Crimley. She was walking along the High Street with him now. 'I'm glad we met,' she said. 'It's such fun being here with you.' Her voice was soft and musical. She looked up into his face. They were happy together, letting the world go by. . . .

'Sorry.'

'Look where you're going, can't you?'

'I'm sorry, I didn't mean to do that.'

—Come on, boy. Come on.

—Head post office, jewellers, Rialto Cinema. What's on at the cinema?

The Thing from Under the Earth. Not a pretty sight! Even the Thing seems to have a girl friend. But she doesn't look very happy. Maybe I'm better looking than *The Thing from Under the Earth.* Just.

—Getting past the centre now. Bank, newsagent, sweet shop, Jeff's Café. Dirty place, Jeff's. The sort of place your parents don't like. Not very busy at the moment. It's used by lorry drivers and workmen. There aren't many around on a Saturday night.

—What about a cup of tea in Jeff's? Your parents don't like Jeff's.

—But your parents aren't here and this is your night out.

—In you go.

. . . You wouldn't bring Barbara to a place like this.

9

2

The boy walked into the café. No one took any notice of him. He found a seat at a table near the window. The café was almost empty. Most of the tables were covered with dirty plates and the remains of meals.

At the counter a girl was laughing with a customer. She pretended to be angry at what he was saying. She was fair-haired with a round face, and wore a white overall. It wasn't very white, either.

'Lynn,' a man's voice called from the back of the café. 'If you've nothing else to do, clear away some of those plates.'

The girl said something that Graham couldn't hear.

'That's right – you tell him,' said the man at the counter. 'Give up the job, dear. Come out on the town with me.'

'Are you going to pay me for it?' asked the girl.

'Money? I don't pay girls to come out with me,' the man said. 'They do it for fun.'

'Find someone who thinks it'll be fun, then!' the girl said.

'Lynn!' called the voice from the back.

'I'm serving a customer,' she answered. She looked in Graham's direction. 'Come up here if you want anything,' she said. 'This isn't an expensive restaurant, you know.'

Graham went up to the counter. 'A cup of tea please,' he said quietly.

'Did you say something?' said the man at the counter in a loud voice. 'You'll have to speak up, son. We're all big boys here.'

'Oh, leave him alone,' the girl said. 'I heard him all right. He's OK – aren't you, dear? He's a customer, Sam Bell, the same as you are.'

She pushed a large cup of tea towards Graham

'Is that all right, love?' she asked.

10

Three men at a back table were leaving. One of them called to Sam as he was going, 'Did you hear that, Sam? First "dear", then "love". The boy's taking your place. You're losing your girl friend.'

'Get lost,' said Sam. He was big, heavy, hard-eyed. He didn't seem amused.

'Now, Sam,' said the girl. 'Don't be like that. It isn't your fault that you haven't got fair hair and glasses, like the boy. . . . Eight pence, love.'

Graham paid. He knew she was teasing Sam, but his face was red.

'No luck for me tonight,' said Sam. He finished his drink and went to the door.

'Nor any other night,' Lynn called after him.

Graham picked up his cup and went back to his seat near the window. Another customer left the café. Graham and the girl were alone. The girl put a coin into the juke-box. She danced a few steps to the music, and smiled at Graham.

—Pretty, maybe. In a way. Nice shape, legs not bad but a little thick. Might be seventeen or eighteen.

—Your mother won't like her.

—So what? Mother doesn't like anything that's young and girl-shaped. Except Beth Edwards and she's just young.

—Pretty, maybe. Good-natured. But not your type, Graham. Certainly not.

'Lynn!' The voice came from the back again. 'What about the dishes?'

'In a minute, Jeff. In a minute.'

The girl came over to Graham. She pushed some dirty cups away and sat on the edge of the table.

'Hi,' she said.

Graham went red and didn't say anything.

'Don't worry about Sam,' she said. 'He's not bad at heart. It's just his way.'

'Oh, I wasn't worried,' Graham said. 'But thanks for what you said.'

'That's nothing. I can look after myself, but you're not used to it. What are you doing here, anyway? I haven't seen you before.'

11

'I just wanted a cup of tea.'

'Are you a student or something?'

'I'm at school here. At the Grammar School.'

'You must be clever to go there.'

'Not really. I find the work hard, but my Dad pushes me. You know what parents are like.'

'No, I don't. My Dad only pushed me once, and that was out of the house.'

'You don't live at home, then?'

'Of course not. My home's in Birmingham. If you can call it a home.'

'You have a room here, then?'

'In a way.'

She took out some cigarettes and offered Graham one. He refused and she took one for herself.

'I think you look clever,' she said. 'Fellows like Sam Bell are jealous, that's the long and the short of it. That's why they try to make fun of you. But I told you, don't worry about them.'

A man came through the green curtain between the café and the kitchen behind it. He was in his thirties, broad, with the build of a fighter, and thick, dark hair. This must be the owner of the café.

The girl was still sitting on the edge of Graham's table. She continued to smoke her cigarette, without hurrying.

'Get the dishes cleared and washed up,' the man said.

'It's not my job. You pay me to serve. Clearing up and washing dishes, that's Arthur's job.'

'It's your job tonight. Arthur's sick.'

'Why don't you do it yourself?'

'So, I pay you to sit around talking to customers while I do all the work. Is that the idea?' He looked quietly at Graham. 'Do you want anything more, son?'

'No, thank you.'

'Well, if you've finished, you can go. This isn't a waiting-room.'

He turned back to the girl. 'Are you going to work, Lynn, or aren't you?'

'All right, all right, Jeff. Keep cool.' Lynn got down from the

12

table and began to work very slowly, carrying dirty plates to the counter.

—You ought to say something, Graham, boy. She spoke up for you a few minutes ago.

—Don't be silly. She has to do what he says. Naturally.

—No, there's something in the air between them. It's like a storm about to break. If she goes on being so slow . . .

'Maybe I can help,' he offered without thinking.

'Maybe you can mind your own business,' said Jeff.

'The boy's done nothing to you,' Lynn said. 'You shouldn't speak to him like that. He's at the Grammar School.'

'What if he is?'

'You can be kinder to him, that's what.'

Jeff stopped, thought for a minute, then said to Graham, 'I don't care who you are. I don't care where you go to school. But you can help if you really want to. We get a lot of customers here, late at night. You can have a free meal. How long can you stay?'

'I can stay as long as I want,' said Graham.

'Ooh, you old night-bird!' the girl said. Graham went red again.

'There, there. Sorry, love,' she said. 'You see, Jeff, you mustn't hurt his feelings.'

'We close at midnight,' Jeff said. 'Can you stay till then?'

'Yes,' said Graham.

'Fifty pence then,' Jeff said. 'But you work for it. Understand? Right. Start now. Take all these dirty things into the kitchen. Wash them, dry them, and put them away. Alice will show you.'

A bell rang and the door from the street opened. Six men came in.

'Here they come,' Jeff said. 'The first of the many.'

In the kitchen Graham found Alice. She was small and thin, in late middle age. Her job was to get the food ready. She worked fast and in silence.

—What will *she* say? Your mother. She won't like it, that's certain. Working in Jeff's Café, of *all* places!

—Why always 'What will Mother say?' She won't know. The

13

news won't get to the west of Ireland! You can do as you like all week. You're free.

—There's no time to think. The place is filling up quickly. Clear the tables, start washing the cups and plates. Lynn's calling for more. Half-dry a few plates, pass them to her quickly, dry the rest. Now Jeff wants the tables cleared again. Hurry round, careful, careful, nearly dropped that lot. Get busy, washing, drying. Lynn still wants clean cups. Can't keep it up. Can't keep it up. Thank God for Alice. She's quick and helps without a word. Washing dishes and frying eggs at the same time.

—Frying. Fried food all night, seen, smelt, eaten. Makes you feel ill. I never want anything fried again. In the front of the café, the air is full of smoke. It makes your eyes water. You get used to it. Lynn's at the counter, not worried, serving all the customers. Laughing at the jokes and making fun of everyone. Giving orders, quick, clever.

—My head's starting to ring. I can't go on much longer at this speed.

—Business is getting slower. Not many people coming in now.

—What a job! It's hell!

—But it's fun at the same time.

—I'm working for money for the first time in my life! What *will* mother say?

—Who cares?

Jeff marched through the café. He turned the OPEN card on the door to CLOSED.

'We'll clean up now,' he said. Graham washed the last cups and plates. Alice and Lynn washed and cleaned the kitchen. Jeff counted the money. They made a fresh cup of tea for themselves and Jeff passed some cigarettes around. Graham smoked with the others.

Jeff gave him a 50p piece. He put it in his pocket without a word.

'Old Arthur will be away for a week,' Jeff said. 'You can come in every night if you want. But you'll have to work a bit faster.'

'He was fine,' said Lynn. 'Much quicker than Arthur.'

'Well, do you want to come in for a week, son?' Jeff asked. 'You can please yourself. You choose.'

'I don't know,' said Graham.

'Oh, come on, love,' said Lynn. 'Say yes for me. I've become quite a fan of yours.'

Once more Graham went red.

'Look at him!' cried Lynn laughing. 'Isn't he sweet? I wonder if you were sweet at his age, Jeff?'

'Jeff was never his age!' said Alice.

'You'll have to pay him well,' Lynn said to Jeff. 'A pound a night – that's fair.'

'It's too much,' said Jeff.

'Go on, you've got the money.'

'You keep out of it, Lynn,' said Jeff. 'All right, son. A pound a night, from eight to twelve-thirty, tomorrow till next Friday. Take it or leave it. Yes or no?'

'He says "Yes",' said Lynn.

'Yes,' said Graham, looking a little worried.

'Right,' Jeff said. 'What's your name? Graham? Graham what?'

'Hollis.'

'I shall call you Prof,' said Lynn. 'You look like a professor with those glasses. But you're nice, Prof. He's nice, isn't he, Alice? I think I could fall for him.'

'You won't make Jeff jealous,' said Alice.

'Jeff?' said Lynn. 'What's Jeff to me?'

Alice laughed but said nothing.

'There, it's time you went home, Prof,' said Lynn. 'Your Mum will wonder where you are, getting back so late.'

'My parents are away all week,' said Graham. He got up, a little shakily.

'You're looking white, love,' said Lynn.

'I'm all right.'

'Shall I see you home, Prof? Don't worry, I won't come in. That's if you don't ask me, of course.'

'Shut up, Lynn!' said Jeff. His voice was angry. 'Off you go, Graham. See you at eight o'clock.'

15

'Goodnight, Prof, love,' said Lynn. Alice said nothing.

'Goodnight,' said Graham. He went out into the empty High Street.

—Yes, it's cold.

—As Mother said.

—Still you've got your coat.

—As Mother said.

—I'm feeling a bit ill. All those smells. That cigarette. The hurry. All *too* new, perhaps.

—You've got a job.

—That's *not* as Mother said.

—A job for a week. At Jeff's Café.

—I can't believe it.

—It's a fact. At Jeff's Café. The sort of place your parents don't like.

He started for home.

3

Graham was sick when he got home. During the night he was sick again, three times. He woke at midday feeling weak and light-headed. Breakfast was bread and butter and a glass of milk. It was a fine September Sunday. He sat in the garden, reading a book.

... He saw her, dark and beautiful. She came round the side of the house towards him. Barbara.

... 'Hullo,' she said. 'You mustn't read on a day like this. Come for a walk in the hills. We'll be alone with the wind and the birds.' Then she saw he wasn't well. 'Oh, you poor thing,' she said. 'You poor, poor, thing. Don't do anything! Let me look after you. ...

—Come on, boy. You may be ill. But not *that* ill. Jeff's Café is real. Barbara isn't. What a fool you were. You agreed to work there all week. The place made you feel sick. The noise, the hurry, the smells. You can't go back there.

—I'm not well enough to go tonight. That's a good excuse.

—Rubbish! You're better already. You ate that bread and butter.

—I think I ought to go.

—That awful place. That awful man, Jeff. That awful Alice who never says a nice word. And that awful girl. Above all, that awful girl.

—She's not so bad.

—She made eyes at you and then laughed at you.

—She spoke up for me.

—Only for fun. You know what your mother will say about her.

—No, and I don't care.

—Not a 'nice' girl. That's it. She's not a 'nice' girl.

—She seemed OK. Anyway, I'm not interested.

17

—You are. You only *say* you aren't. She's not a 'nice' girl.

—Don't forget they're paying me a pound a night.

—So what? You've plenty of money. You don't care about the money. You're thinking of the girl.

—I'm not.

—Forget her. She's not your type. Her legs are too thick.

—Perhaps I won't go.

—That's better.

—Perhaps I will.

He walked slowly down the High Street. Jeff's café was on the other side of the street. He looked across at it. The café looked dirty and badly painted. It was eight o'clock.

... It was a fine September evening. 'I quite like this little town,' she said. 'When I'm with someone nice, anyway. Like you. Let's walk down to the river. We can look up at the stars.' Barbara took his arm and smiled up into his face....

—Now then, Graham. Come down to earth. Are you going to Jeff's tonight or not?

—A promise is a promise.

—That awful place. That awful girl.

—She spoke up for you, didn't she?

—That awful girl.

Graham crossed the road and pushed open the café door.

They were busy. Graham started washing cups and plates. Lynn smiled at him. She continued to serve and talk to the customers. Graham cleared the tables and washed the dishes again.

Alice was silent in the kitchen. Jeff was at his desk. Then he got up and put on his jacket.

'I'll be back in ten minutes,' he said.

Alice put an egg and two sausages on a plate. Without a word, she gave the plate to Graham. He found he was hungry, and ate.

'Hi, Prof,' said Lynn. 'How are you?'

'Not so bad.'

'You're quicker tonight, aren't you?'

'I'm learning.'

Then she was serving again. Taking orders and answering back. Graham went on clearing tables, washing plates, drying them. Clearing tables, washing plates, drying them ... the customers came and went. Jeff returned.

Time passed quickly. It was midnight. Jeff turned the notice to CLOSED. They cleaned up, made themselves a pot of tea. Smoked.

—She hasn't said much tonight. Perhaps she's thinking of something else. She hasn't made eyes at me. She hasn't even made fun of me!

—Do you want her to?

—No but last night she wanted me to stay. She asked me to stay.

—You didn't have to come.

—Maybe she's not interested in me. She's playing around.

—Of course she's not interested in you.

—But she *seemed* interested.

Jeff paid him a pound. He took it and went home.

Monday.

—It's not so busy tonight. Eight o'clock and the place is empty. Tables cleared, plates and cups washed. Jeff's sitting at his little desk in the corner. A chance to talk to Lynn.

'Hi, Lynn.'

'Hi, Prof. How's it going?'

'All right.'

She put a coin in the juke-box and danced a step or two to the music.

'Want to dance, Prof?'

'There isn't much space, is there?'

'I've danced in less. Oh, hell, here comes Casanova! Sam Bell.'

Graham recognized the big, heavy man who now came in. Sam Bell walked shakily to the counter.

'Is he drunk?' Graham asked.

'No. He's had two or three, maybe, but he's not drunk. Hi, Sam.'

'Hello, sweetheart. What are you doing tonight?'

'Working.'

'You always say that. Come out on the town with me.'

'You always say that.'

'There's plenty more I could say. Here, listen,' He put his lips to Lynn's ear. She gave a little laugh.

'Certainly not,' she said. 'Cup of tea, Sam?'

'Yes, that'll do. Oh, there's our silent young friend.' He turned to Graham. 'Pleased to see you again.'

Graham said nothing. He cleaned an already clean table with a cloth.

'Great little talker, isn't he,' Sam said to Lynn. 'Aren't you speaking to me tonight, sir?'

'Good evening,' Graham said.

'Good evening,' said Sam copying Graham's voice exactly. He turned to Lynn. 'I don't think the young man likes me.'

Lynn and Graham were silent.

'And do you know what?' said Sam. 'I think the young man should be careful. Because I might decide that I don't like him.'

Sam Bell had very large hands. He closed one of them, the right one. 'Come here, mister,' he said to Graham.

'Take your tea, Sam, and sit down,' said Lynn.

Sam looked away from Graham. Suddenly he seemed to forget all about him.

'You look lovely tonight, Lynn,' he said.

'I always do.'

'Of course you do. Here, you, mister. Shall I tell you something? She always looks lovely. Always. Without fail. Don't you think she looks lovely, mister?'

Graham went red.

'Go on, tell me,' Sam said. 'Don't you think she looks lovely?'

'Eight pence,' said Lynn. 'One cup of tea, eight pence.'

She put out her hand for the money. Sam took hold of it, and pulled her from behind the counter. He put an arm round her.

'Stop it, Sam,' she said. She looked angry, not afraid. 'That's enough of that.'

20

'Oh, no, it isn't,' said Sam. He put his head close to hers. She tried to pull away. Sam's large hand lay across the front of her dress. Anger shook Graham. Suddenly he felt himself jump forward and hit Sam on the arm. It was a useless attack. And without effect on Sam.

There was complete surprise on Sam's face and on Lynn's.

Sam pulled his arm away from Lynn. He looked straight into Graham's eyes. Graham was himself again, shaking with fear.

—Have you lost your mind? It's nothing to do with you. Nothing.

—I had to do something.

—He's lifting his hand. He's going to hit you.

'Jeff,' cried Lynn very loudly.

Jeff appeared in the doorway from the kitchen. 'What's happening?' he asked quickly. Sam's hands dropped to his sides. He still seemed very surprised.

'Out!' said Jeff.

'It wasn't me, it was him,' complained Sam.

'Out!' said Jeff again.

Sam was taller and heavier than Jeff. But Jeff's voice contained the bite of command. Jeff was a fighter. Sam opened his mouth to argue, then he closed it again. He turned round and went out angrily.

'Did you hit him?' said Jeff to Graham.

'Yes,' said Graham.

'Why?'

'The Prof – Graham, I mean – thought Sam was attacking me,' Lynn said.

'And was he?'

'Not really. He was just having some fun. You know Sam. But Graham thought he was.'

'You can go, too,' Jeff said to Graham. 'And don't come back. I'm not having any fights in here.'

'He did it for me, Jeff,' said Lynn.

'I don't care why he did it.'

'Listen, Jeff,' said Lynn. 'It was sudden. The boy didn't understand. He'll know another time.'

'There won't be another time. He's finished here.'

21

'If he goes, I go.'

'You know very well you won't.'

'I'll go,' said Graham. His legs were weak. He sat down on the nearest chair.

Two or three customers came in. Jeff changed his mind.

'I'll give you one more chance,' he said. 'But next time you'll be out. You'll be through that door before your feet touch the ground.'

Jeff disappeared towards the back.

'Poor old Prof,' Lynn said. 'You do look white! Here, have a cup of tea.'

Graham drank it and began to feel better.

'You ought to be more careful, Prof,' said Lynn. 'You won't live long as a fighter. Sam Bell could eat you for breakfast!'

Graham managed a smile.

'Still, it was as good as the television,' Lynn went on. 'The way you jumped in and hit him.'

'I'm glad you enjoyed the show,' Graham said heavily. 'I think I'll go home now.'

'No, don't go,' she said. 'I forgot about your feelings then. Listen, love, I thought you were great. I did really. Nobody has ever looked after me before. Here, Prof, I mean Graham. Look up.'

Graham looked up. She bent down and gave him a quick kiss. 'There,' she said. 'That's for being a good boy.'

The café was filling up. Both Lynn and Graham were soon busy. Time flew. Jeff turned the OPEN notice to CLOSED. They were sitting in the kitchen drinking tea and smoking.

'Do you feel all right now, love?' Lynn said to Graham. 'Not sick or anything?'

'I'm OK,' said Graham.

'You were brave. That's what you were. Brave,' said Lynn. She reached across the table and took Graham's hand. She held it between her own warm hands. 'Nobody has ever looked after me before,' she said. 'Never in my whole life.'

'I thought you could look after yourself,' said Alice.

'That's not the point,' Lynn said. She was still holding

Graham's hand. 'You're a love, aren't you? Nice looking, isn't he, Jeff? Eh, Jeff? I said he's nice looking, isn't he?'

Jeff remained silent.

'I expect you've got lots of girl friends,' Lynn went on. 'Wait, I'm interested. Have you got a girl friend?'

Graham went red once more.

'He has!' Lynn was laughing. 'He has! Look at his face! Go on, Prof, tell us about her. What's her name? What does she look like?'

'Shut up, Lynn, can't you?' said Jeff.

'No, I can't,' said Lynn. 'Where is she now, Prof? Does she know you're working here? Bring her in to see us.'

'Well,' Graham began, 'she doesn't live around here. Her name's Barbara. She lives on the south coast. I met her when I was on holiday.' He stopped.

'She's dark,' he said. 'She's got long dark hair and a lovely soft voice.'

'I'm jealous,' said Lynn.

'I told you to shut up, Lynn,' Jeff said. 'It's time we went.' He stood up.

'I'll come part of the way home with you,' Lynn said to Graham.

'There's no need,' he said.

'Go on, Prof, you're not afraid of me, are you?' She was putting on her coat. Out in the street she took his arm.

'Tell me more about Barbara,' she said.

'Look,' Graham said. 'We've talked a lot about me and her. What about you? Have you got a boy friend?'

'Well – yes and no.'

'What's his name?'

'It doesn't matter to you, Prof, does it? You've already got Barbara.'

'I've told you plenty. You could tell me a bit.'

'It's time I was going,' she said.

'Where do you live?'

'Oh, I know my way home.'

'I hope you do! That wasn't the question,' Graham said. 'I ought to see you home, instead of you seeing me home.'

23

'I haven't got far to go.'

'How far?'

'If you must know,' she said, 'I live over the café.'

'Oh,' Graham said quietly. Then, 'Where does Jeff live?'

'That's his business. Ask him.'

'I see,' said Graham.

'Do you?' she said quickly. 'Well, it's time I was going. See you. Goodnight.'

'Goodnight.'

He walked a few metres. She came running after him. He turned. She held his arm. 'You were lovely,' she said. 'Thank you. But don't do it again. I like you best in one piece. And listen. *Never* argue with Jeff. *Never*. Do you understand?'

'Yes,' he said. 'I suppose so.'

She kissed him, quickly. On the lips.

'Goodnight, Prof, love,' she said.

4

Tuesday morning. A postcard, with a view of Bantry Bay.

'Having quite a good time. The weather has been very wet. We are going to visit Glengariff tomorrow. Let's hope it's a bit drier. Look after yourself. Eat good meals. Love, Mum and Dad.' It was written by his mother.

—Hell. I should have sent her a letter yesterday. I'll write one this morning. She'll be angry if she doesn't hear from me.

'Dear Mum and Dad,

'I am very well and looking after myself. I have done lots of work.'

—That's not true! You haven't done any.

'I am eating good food and going for walks. There's a film called *The Thing from Under the Earth*. I might go and see it with John Wyatt.'

—Might you?

—Well, there's nothing to stop me. I might.

—And you might not.

'Don't worry about me, I'm fine. Looking forward to seeing you on Saturday. Lots of love, Graham.'

—Nothing about the job.

—Of course not. I'll never tell them about it.

—Because they'll be angry?

—No. Because I must live my own life. They don't have to know everything.

—It's the girl, isn't it? That awful girl.

—She's all right. She spoke up for me. She kissed me twice.

—A fine story you told her. About Barbara.

—Yes. She believed it. She even sounded jealous. Jealous of Barbara, who isn't real! A girl of air!

... They were walking together on the hills. It was a cool, grey, stormy day. Her dark hair flew out in the wind. There was

25

colour in her face. It was wild up there, wild and beautiful. She ran ahead of him. He ran too, and caught her hand. They ran together hand in hand. And then she knew something. He didn't tell her, she just knew. She got away from him and ran out of sight. ...

—Barbara, come back, come back.

—Nothing there. The dream has died. Gone.

—A girl of air. Gone.

—A girl of flesh and blood. She kissed me, twice. She's real. She's alive.

'Come right in,' said Alice. 'I need you.' Graham took off his jacket.

'What's the matter? Where's everyone?'

'There's only you and me. And a minute ago there was only me. To do the work of four. So get started. You can serve.'

'What's happened? Has she . . . gone?'

'Of course not. She's having a night out with Jeff. She told him it was time they went out. So they went out.'

'I don't understand.'

'Easy enough, isn't it?'

'No.'

'Then write me a letter. Now, start serving those customers.'

Graham was busy, serving and clearing the tables. It was a long evening. Without Lynn, the place seemed lifeless. There were no jokes, no laughter. Just silent men eating and drinking and leaving.

When Alice turned the OPEN sign to CLOSED the café was empty. She and Graham sat at the kitchen table in the back.

'Does she – do they – often go out like this?' he asked.

'What does it matter to you? You'll get paid as usual.'

'It's more work for you and me,' he said.

'I'm always doing more work,' Alice said. 'But *she* doesn't. There's plenty of noise if *she* has more to do. Of course he always gives in. That's the difference between being her age and being mine.'

'But I said, does it often happen? Does she often go out with Jeff?'

'You could say that,' said Alice.

A minute went by before she answered his question. Then she said: 'Not often. When she's had enough. It's a seven-day week here. You need a break sometimes. I should know. I'm supposed to get my day off. I can't remember the last time I got it.'

Then they arrived. Jeff was wearing a suit. Lynn had on a short coat and a dress. Her perfume fought with the smell of the café and won. She looked two or three years older than usual. They both seemed angry. Jeff went back to his desk. Alice pushed a cup of tea in front of Lynn and said, 'You're not speaking to each other again, eh?'

Lynn smoked a cigarette and didn't answer. Her eyes became softer when she saw Graham.

'Hi, Prof,' she said.

'Hi, Lynn,' said Graham.

'How's my old Prof? I'll miss you when you stop coming here, love. I will, really.'

'Thank you,' said Graham.

'I'm sure *you* know how to look after a girl,' she said. 'But I know someone who doesn't. He takes a girl to a club and spends half the time drinking with his friends. The other half he's giving some other girl the "glad eye". Now you don't do that, do you?'

Graham didn't answer.

'Do you?' she continued.

'N-no,' said Graham.

'Of course you don't. If you take a girl out you look after her. Do you hear that, Jeff,' she called out. 'The Prof knows how to look after a girl.'

'Shut up, Lynn,' said Jeff from his desk.

Lynn made a face in his direction. Then she spoke to Graham. 'I'm jealous of that girl of yours; what was her name?'

'Barbara.'

'Lucky girl. I hope she knows how lucky she is.' Lynn put out her cigarette. 'Poor boy, she's all those miles away. I'm sure you want to get your arm round her.'

Graham went red and didn't answer.

'He wants to get his arm round a girl,' Lynn called loudly.
'Well, go on, tell him to get it round you,' said Jeff.
'That's not such a bad idea,' said Lynn.

Wednesday night.

Lynn wasn't speaking to anyone. Not to Jeff. Not to Graham. Not even, at first, to the customers. She splashed tea on the counter. She banged plates on the tables. She took money without a please or a thank you. She had an angry look for everyone.

But this became a joke. Customers tried to make her laugh. She found it harder and harder not to smile. At last she broke down and laughed. The air in the café grew lighter. Customers stayed. They joked with Lynn and bought more food. At closing time the café was still half-full. Jeff hurried out the last customers.

Lynn fell angrily silent again. Graham got up to go. Nobody answered his 'Goodnight.'

But at the doorway, Lynn caught him up.

'I'll walk you home,' she said.

'What's the matter?' Graham asked.

'Oh, nothing. Or everything.'

'Well, it can't be nothing. You've been angry all night. Tell me about it.'

'Don't worry, Prof. It's nothing to do with you.'

'Why are you walking me home, then?'

'I don't know. I like being with you, Prof. Graham, I mean. You're gentle, that's what it is. Not like *him*.'

'Jeff?'

'Yes, Jeff.'

'What's the trouble with Jeff?'

'Well, what do you think of him?'

'I haven't really thought,' Graham said. 'He knows what he's doing. He's a hard man.'

'You can say that again! He knows what he's doing all right. And he's hard. You won't find anyone harder. Listen, Graham, who brings the customers into the café?'

'You do.'

28

'Right. Then why is he so awful to me!'

'I don't know what he does to you.'

'No, I suppose you don't. And I'm not going to tell you, either. You're only a boy. But I'll tell you this. It's bad, really bad.'

'Why don't you leave, then?'

'It's not as easy as that. For a start, I live above the café. Where else can I go?'

'It's not that difficult, is it?'

'No. But – oh, I don't know, Gray. It's me as well. I left home two years ago. I don't have anyone but him. He's a great fellow sometimes, when he wants to be. But that's not often, now. He thinks he's got me where he wants me. And maybe he has.'

Graham was silent. They turned the corner into his road.

'I still think you should leave,' he said at last.

'Oh, I don't know, Prof. Sometimes I don't know if I'm coming or going.'

'I'm sorry,' Graham said.

'I know. I can feel you are. Why aren't there more people like you? Well, I suppose there are, but I never meet them . . . Is this your house?'

'Yes.'

'What does your dad do?'

'He's an accountant.'

'Not bad, eh? Like being a doctor. And what will you do?'

'I suppose I'll be an accountant with him. If I pass my exams.'

'Of course you'll pass them. You're clever.'

'Not very.'

'Clever and nice too. Come here.' She kissed him. 'I ought to really kiss you,' she said. She laughed. 'But you need some sleep! Oh, well. Off you go now. Time for bed and dreamland. Think beautiful thoughts . . . Did you say something?'

'No.'

'Oh, well . . . Goodnight, Prof, love. God bless.'

Thursday morning. Another postcard from Ireland. This time with a view of Killarney.

'We phoned last night but no answer. Where were you? Hope to get your letter at Connemara tomorrow. We drove round the Ring of Kerry today. Hope all is well. Love, Mum and Dad.'

—Hell. You didn't post that letter. It's too late now. They won't get it. They never said they were going to phone from Ireland! How many times have they rung already? You'll be in big trouble next week.

—It's all because of working at Jeff's. I'm glad it's nearly over. Tonight and tomorrow night. Then you've finished.

—Trouble or not, I'll miss it in a way.

—You'll miss her, you mean.

—All right, I'll miss *her*. And she'll miss me. She said so.

—You should stay away from there. Think of Jeff. How close is she to Jeff? You don't know, but you have a good idea. A very good idea. You don't want to argue with Jeff.

—She's had enough of Jeff.

—Yes, for the moment.

—Not for the moment. For always. Poor Lynn.

—How can she get away from him, anyway?

—I don't know. I wish I could help.

'I like being with you, Prof. You're gentle. Not like *him*.'

—Poor Lynn, what can I do for you?

5

Thursday night.

No Lynn.

'Alice, where is she?'

'Not helping *us*!'

Jeff is at the counter, serving. The customers don't like it. There's no joking or laughing. It's been a busy night, but it's slowing down now. Two or three customers are talking over their tea-cups at a corner table. All the other tables are cleared, all the dishes are washed. Jeff is still at the counter, by himself, reading a magazine.

'He's not talking to us tonight, is he, Alice?'

'He's angry.'

'About – Lynn?'

'Ssssh. Not so loud. He can hear you out there. Let's have a cup of tea before they start coming in again. And what about a drop of something in it?' A quick smile crossed her face. She took a small flat bottle from her bag. She emptied it into the two cups. She and Graham sat down at the kitchen table.

The door from the living-room opened quietly.

'Well,' said Alice. 'So you've decided to appear after all.'

Lynn put her finger to her lips. She was dressed to go out. She wore a short coat and carried a weekend bag.

She pointed to the other end of the kitchen towards Jeff's desk.

'He's not there, he's in the café,' Alice said quietly.

Lynn walked carefully past them. Then she was at Jeff's desk, opening and shutting it.

'Here, what are you doing?' said Alice. 'Come out of there.'

Lynn didn't answer.

'Are you mad?' said Alice. 'Jeff will kill you.'

'He'll have to catch me first,' Lynn said. Then Jeff came in

31

from the café, stepping lightly, like a fighter. Lynn turned. She was holding her bag in front of her with both hands. Jeff didn't move.

'Come here,' he said quietly.

Lynn stayed where she was. 'Lynn,' Jeff said. His eyes were small and cold. 'Come here when I tell you.'

Suddenly Graham felt afraid.

'Go to hell,' Lynn said. Her voice shook.

'Where are you going, Lynn?'

'Mind your own business.'

'What were you doing in there, Lynn?'

'Mind your own business.'

'What were you doing in there, Lynn?'

No answer.

'What have you got in your bag, Lynn?'

'The money you owe me! Four weeks' money!'

'You're not thinking of leaving, are you, Lynn?'

'Yes. I am!'

'Don't do that, Lynn.' Quietly.

'I'll do as I like.'

'Come here, Lynn.' Quieter still. She didn't move.

'Come here!' Jeff shot the words out like a gun. With small, slow steps, Lynn walked towards him. She looked like a child waiting to be hit. Then suddenly, she ran past Jeff and through the door into the café. Jeff jumped up to go after her. Graham, white-faced and shaking, stood in the way.

'Move,' Jeff said. They heard Lynn running through the café.

'*Move*,' Jeff said again.

'No,' said Graham. The street door crashed behind Lynn. Graham was still in the way.

—He'll kill you.

—I must stay. I've got no choice. Every second helps her.

Jeff raised a hand. Then stopped. He picked Graham up and threw him out of the way. Graham hit a table. The table crashed against the wall. Leaving Graham sitting on the floor, Jeff ran through the café and out into the street.

'Get out of here while you've got the chance,' said Alice. 'God, you're lucky. If Jeff hit you . . .'

32

There was a back door. Alice opened it. 'Goodbye,' she said. 'Don't come back here tomorrow. Go home and stay home.'

Graham found himself in a back street. He rested against a wall. His legs felt weak.

—No sound from the café. Did she get away?

—Keep away now, boy. You can't do anything about Jeff. Next time you won't live to tell the story.

—Poor Lynn, what can I do for her?

—Nothing, boy, nothing.

His legs felt stronger. He began to walk home along the side streets. He came to the road which led to his house.

Someone came out from behind a tree and Graham jumped.

'Lynn!' He cried in surprise. 'You escaped!'

'I did,' she said. She sounded tired.

'Will he still be looking for you?'

'I don't know. Maybe, maybe not. But he won't come this way. He'll probably go down to the station. He thinks I'll leave Crimley.'

'What are you going to do, then?'

'You tell me, Prof. I need someone like you to help me. I do everything wrong.'

'We can't talk out here, can we?'

'Your house is along this street, isn't it? And your parents are away.'

'Yes. Until tomorrow night.'

'I'm not thinking about tomorrow night. I'm thinking about the next half-hour.'

'All right. But don't let Mrs Grimshaw see you!'

'Who?'

'Our next door neighbour.'

'You're not a child.'

'I am to her and my parents.'

'She won't see us in the dark.'

'She sees everything!'

But there was no sign of life in the Grimshaw house. Graham led Lynn up the drive and into the kitchen.

'I'll make a cup of tea,' said Graham. He lit the gas. 'This feels just like Jeff's,' he said and he put the kettle on.

'Oh, no, it doesn't. This is a home. It's completely different. Do you mind if I look round?'

She disappeared into the hall. Graham found her ten minutes later. She was sitting in a big chair in the living-room, trying it out, as if it was in a shop.

'You're got a lovely place here,' she said.

'There's nothing unusual about it,' Graham said. 'Come and have some tea.'

Back in the kitchen Lynn lit a cigarette and sat down. She seemed quite happy.

'Hullo, Prof, love,' she said.

'Hullo, Lynn,' he said, 'love.'

'That's better. Hey, Graham. What are you looking at? Have you just noticed I'm a girl?'

'It's not difficult to notice.'

'Aren't you sweet!' she said. 'I love the way you say things.'

'Listen,' Graham said. 'An hour ago you walked out of Jeff's café. You must decide what you're going to do now.'

'I suppose I must,' she said. She didn't sound worried. 'Have you got any ideas, Prof?'

Graham shook his head. 'Don't you have a family to go to?' he asked.

'My family live in Birmingham. I haven't heard from them since I left. And if you want to know, I don't care if I never see them again.'

'Then where are you going to go?' Graham asked.

'My life's not like yours,' she said. 'You must live and let live, Prof.'

'I suppose so,' Graham said. He was silent. Then he said, 'You've had lots of boy friends, haven't you, Lynn?'

'Lots.'

There was silence for two or three minutes.

'OK,' Lynn said quietly. 'You want me to leave. All right, I'm just going.'

'But going where?'

'What's it got to do with you?'

'I worry about you, Lynn. Listen, you can stay here tonight, if you like. But tomorrow my parents are coming home. If they find a girl in the house, I don't know what'll happen.'

'I won't stay where I'm not wanted.'

'You are wanted, Lynn.'

'Oh, Prof, don't worry. I'll be all right. You shouldn't ask questions. We were happy till you started asking questions.'

'We're still happy,' said Graham. 'You'll have to stay. We'll talk about things in the morning.'

'Before they arrive, hey?'

'Yes. They won't be early. The crossing from Ireland is at tea-time. They won't get here till tomorrow night.'

'Gray! What was that noise?'

'I didn't hear anything.'

'It sounded like a car. Here, Gray! Suppose they're a day early?'

'Oh, God! Not that!' They heard a key turning.

'It's them!' Graham said. He and Lynn looked at each other. Then they looked at the window.

'Can I get out through there?' Lynn asked.

'No, it's too small,' Graham said.

Mrs Hollis's voice called from the hall. 'Graham! Graham! You're not in bed, then?'

'There's no time to do anything . . .' Graham said. His face was white.

The voice called again. 'Graham! We're back! Graham!' The footsteps came nearer. One second to go and nothing to be done.

'Sorry, Prof, love,' Lynn said.

6

'Of course I believe you,' Mr Hollis said. 'Your story sounds true. I quite understand Miss – er Miss . . .'

'Lynn.'

'Miss Lynn.'

'No, just Lynn.'

'Your mother didn't really mean what she said, Graham.'

'She shouldn't have said it, then!'

'She's had a difficult week. All that rain and no letter from you. Then there was trouble with the car yesterday. You must try to understand.'

'Why can't *she* try to understand?'

'Don't speak about your mother in that voice, please.'

'There, there,' said Lynn. 'I'm the cause of all this trouble. I said I'm sorry. And now if you don't mind, I'll be going.'

'Going where?'

'To my Dad's house in Birmingham,' Lynn said.

Graham looked at her but said nothing.

'It's nearly half-past eleven,' Mr Hollis said. 'You won't get a train out of Crimley tonight.' He thought for a moment. 'We can't leave you on the street. I think we ought to give you a bed. I'll ask my wife.' Mr Hollis went out.

'He'll have a rough time with that idea,' said Graham.

'Hasn't your mum said enough,' Lynn said.

'Enough? She hasn't started yet! She'll begin again tomorrow, and the day after and all next week. I'll never hear the end of it.'

Mrs Hollis came in, her lips pressed together. She didn't look at Lynn or Graham. She spoke as if to a third person.

'I'll make up a bed in the living-room,' she said. 'You can help me if you wish.'

'Oh, sure,' Lynn said.

'I'll come and help too,' said Graham.

'You needn't,' his mother said.

'I will. I want to hear what you say to Lynn. She's had enough from you and so have I.'

'There's no need to worry. I've finished talking to this — person.'

'Oh, God. Just let me take my bag and go,' said Lynn.

'No!' said Graham.

Mr Hollis came back. 'Now, now,' he said. 'This isn't easy for any of us. Let's try to behave like adults. We can give you a bed tonight, er — Lynn. And tomorrow morning we'll see you on to the train for Birmingham.'

'And now she can help me make the bed,' said Mrs Hollis coldly.

Lynn followed her from the room. Mr Hollis closed the door behind them and sat down at the table. 'Now listen carefully to me, young man,' he said to Graham. 'I'm not going to ask you any questions. And I won't speak about this again. But I do just want to say something. You will *not*, I repeat, *not*, go around with that type of girl, ever again. Not while you live here.'

'What do you mean "that type of girl"?'

'You know very well what I mean.'

'Lynn's all right.'

'Perhaps to some people she is not all right. I've told you time and time again. In our business it's important to know the "right" people. And it's also important to recognize the "wrong" people.'

'I could take Lynn anywhere. And it isn't *our* business. It's your business.'

'It'll be yours, too, Graham. You must work hard and pass those exams. As I know you can.'

'I'll always be in your shadow. Always. You want me to pass my exams and go to college. Then I'll enter the company. You'll be watching all the time. What a life I'm going to have!'

'I've always been fair to you, Graham. . . .'

'Oh, yes! You only want to say who I should meet and what I'll do for the rest of my life. That's all.'

'Now, Graham, you're not a child any more. You're nearly

seventeen. You're becoming interested in – in the other sex. I was young myself once, so I know. It's quite natural. But just be more careful, that's all. That girl is not *our* sort. Don't pretend you don't know what I mean.'

'I know only too well!' said Graham.

Mrs Hollis came in again. She was carrying a small silver cup and a number of other valuables. They all came from the living-room.

'Mother!' cried Graham. 'What are you doing with those?'

'You can't be too careful,' said Mrs Hollis. She put them in the back of a cupboard.

'You didn't let her *see* you?'

'I made sure she saw me,' Mrs Hollis said with feeling. 'Now she knows exactly what we think of her!'

'I'll never forget this,' Graham said. 'Never. I might forget the things you said. But not this.'

Suddenly he was crying. 'I hate you. I hate you.'

—Your mother will be awake. Dad won't. But *she* will. Her eyes wide open, looking up into the dark. Seeing her boy leaving her. She'll be lying there thinking, thinking.

—She's jealous. You can't really hate her, can you?

—Yes. For moving the silver.

—What about her life? Married to your father.

—And your life working for him? Hollis & Son, small town accountants. You're the son. Get married to a nice girl like Beth Edwards. Have a son of your own. After twenty years, it's still Hollis and Son. You're Hollis, he's the son. Keep him in order. See he does his work and passes his exams. Keep him away from 'that type of girl'.

—That type of girl. Lynn.

—Hell! She's a woman. Not a Beth Edwards going to school every day. And not a girl of air, like Barbara.

—Lynn's all on her own. Nowhere to go. What is she going to do?

—She might go back to Jeff.

—Back to Jeff? Why should she go back to Jeff? He doesn't

38

love her. Or anybody or anything. Those small, cold eyes; that small, cold voice.

—But does *she* love *him*? 'He's a great fellow, sometimes', she said. What did she mean by that?

—Face the fact, boy. You love Lynn yourself, don't you? You don't want her to go to Birmingham. Or to London. Or back to Jeff. Least of all, back to Jeff.

—Poor Lynn. What can I do for you?

—Anything. I'd do anything in the world for you if I could.

He was nearly asleep when he heard a noise outside his door. He sat up in bed. The door opened quietly.

'Hi,' she breathed.

'Lynn! You must go back to bed. My mother won't be asleep.'

'Poor old Prof.'

'If she hears anything she'll be in here like a shot!'

'All right, Gray,' Lynn said quietly. 'I just came to say goodbye to you, that's all. In case I don't get another chance.'

She was kissing him, long and deeply. He thought suddenly of his mother. Then he didn't think at all. He reached after Lynn as she pulled away.

'No. Remember what you said. Goodnight, Prof, love. God bless.'

'The young *lady*,' said Mrs Hollis, 'is still asleep.' She put a lot of meaning into the word 'lady.'

'Then we ought to wake her up,' said Mr Hollis. 'She must catch that train to Birmingham.'

'I'll take her a cup of tea,' Graham offered.

'Oh, no you won't. I'll have her out of there without any cups of tea,' said Mrs Hollis, and she left the room.

Graham and his father could hear voices in the next room. Mrs Hollis returned. 'Well, I got her out of bed,' she said loudly.

Lynn came in, her eyes heavy.

'Good morning, Lynn,' said Mr Hollis brightly.

39

'Hello,' said Lynn. She wasn't completely awake. 'Has anybody got a cigarette?'

'We don't smoke in this house.'

'There's some in my bag. Go and get it, Gray.'

'I'll get your bag,' said Mrs Hollis. 'If you can't get it yourself.' Lynn pulled a face.

'Do you want anything to eat?' Mr Hollis asked.

Lynn shook her head. 'No,' she said. 'Not at this time of day. Just a cup of tea and a smoke. That's all I want.'

Mrs Hollis banged the bag down in front of her. Lynn lit a cigarette. She sat and smoked in silence.

'I think you ought to get ready now. You must catch that train,' said Mr Hollis.

Lynn was in the bathroom for a long time. She appeared at last carrying her weekend bag. She seemed brighter.

'Well,' she said, looking round at the three faces, 'here we go.'

'You come as well, Graham,' said Mr Hollis. 'I have to be at work at half-past nine. You can see Lynn on to the train.'

Mr Hollis stopped the car in front of Crimley station.

'You'll just catch it,' he said. 'Goodbye, Lynn. I hope all goes well for you.'

'Thanks for everything,' Lynn said.

'I wondered . . .' Mr Hollis went on. He took some money out. 'I wondered if a little money might help . . .?'

'I've got all I need,' said Lynn. Her voice was hard. 'You don't have to pay me to go away.'

7

'I think I've missed the train,' said Lynn.

'No, you haven't,' said Graham. 'There's still two minutes to go. You'll catch it, if you hurry. Here – let me carry your bag.'

'It's not heavy. Just leave it to me. You don't have to stay.'

'We'll have to be quick.'

'I don't feel like running.'

'But Lynn . . .'

'There'll be plenty more trains, won't there?'

'Well, yes, I suppose so.'

'Do you have to report to your Dad? To say that you saw me leave Crimley?'

'No, it's not that, Lynn. It's just that – well, I care about you. And you *have* missed the train now.'

'Oh, Prof, love,' Lynn said. 'You look so worried. Here, sit down. You can stay with me for five minutes if you like. And then I want you to go home and forget the whole thing. Now, why don't you think about something nice? Like Barbara?'

'Barbara?'

'Don't say you've forgotten about your girl friend!'

'Oh, yes. Barbara.'

'When will you see her again?'

'I – oh, I don't know.'

'You must want to see her.'

'I – oh – listen, Lynn, there never *was* any Barbara. She isn't real.'

'What? Do you mean you made her up?'

'Yes. I haven't got a girl friend. I never did have.'

'Poor Prof,' Lynn said. 'Poor old Prof!'

'I've only got *them*. My father and mother. They'll never let me go. Just think of it. I'll live in Crimley for the rest of my life. The only way to escape is to leave home.'

41

'Don't do that. It can be lonely.'

'I *will* do it one of these days, Lynn. Sometimes I hate them. Like now. I know I shouldn't talk this way, but I can't help it. My mother hiding the valuables. My father offering you money. It's awful.'

'But you can't change them, can you? You've got to learn to live with them. Like I do with Jeff.'

'Like what?'

'Hey, Graham! Are you all right?'

'You *are* going back to him, then! That's why you wanted to miss the train!'

'Well ...'

'Don't!' Graham said. 'Don't go back to Jeff!'

'I'll have to, love. I thought about it in bed last night. I didn't want to tell you. It just came out. If I go home, my Dad will throw me out again. And I know Jeff. I can manage him.'

'You could go somewhere different. Make a fresh start.'

'Not alone. No. That's not me, love. You don't understand. I have to be with somebody.'

'But do you *love* Jeff?'

'I'm used to him.'

'That doesn't sound much good,' Graham said. 'Oh, Lynn, why don't we go away, together?'

'What?'

'Just think. I'll get away from my parents. You'll get away from Jeff.'

'Yes. Just think. And think again.'

'But Lynn. *Could* we?

'Graham, love! Aren't you nice? But silly. Yes, I want to... I'm not sure. But we can't.'

'Why not?'

'You know why not.'

'Lynn, listen, I love you. Let's just get on a train and go. Anywhere.'

'Graham, you're lovely but you've got no sense. We haven't any money.'

'I have money, Lynn. I've got over a hundred pounds in the post-office. And twelve pounds at home. I can get it easily.'

'And what will you tell your mother? "I'm running away with Lynn"?'

'I'll think of something to tell her.'

'Look, Graham. If you just want to get your arm around a girl ...'

'I don't just want to get my arm around a girl. I want *you*.'

'It won't last. Anyway your parents will stop it.'

'How could we make it last?' Graham said. 'Hey, Lynn! Why don't we get *married*? They couldn't stop us then!

'What?' she said. Then she was laughing. 'Graham, love,' she said. 'Graham, sweetheart. Are you asking me to marry you?'

'Yes.'

'Well, it's a great day. You're the first. Nobody's ever asked me before. Come here and let me kiss you. . . . No, don't eat me up in the middle of a railway station! Listen, love. Don't make a habit of saying that to a girl. She might say yes!'

'Well, say yes! That's what I want. I mean it, Lynn.'

'Prof, love, I won't do it to you. What about your future? Your exams?'

'I'm not interested in them. Accountancy – it's just adding up numbers. There are other jobs. I'm ready to work.'

'Graham, how old are you?'

'Seventeen next month. How old are you?'

'Eighteen.'

'Only a year older than me.'

'A year in time, maybe. But I'm years and years older than you, really. I've been around, Graham, you haven't.'

'Why did you ask, anyway?'

'Well I can do what I like. I'm grown up by law. You're not – you're under eighteen. You can't get married at your age. Your parents have to agree . . . maybe it's a good thing.'

'I could get married in Scotland,' Graham said. 'The law is different there; you can get married at sixteen. Why don't we go to Scotland? Why don't we run away to Gretna Green?'

Silence.

'Why don't we, Lynn?'

Still silence.

43

'You've heard of Gretna Green, haven't you, Lynn? The first village in Scotland. Where people run off to be married.'

'Yes, Graham! I've heard of Gretna Green!'

'Well, then?'

'When I was young, I dreamed of running off to Gretna Green,' Lynn said slowly. 'I thought it sounded beautiful. A lovely old village. Marriage. And me, Lynn, marrying somebody tall, dark and good-looking.'

'I'm tall,' Graham said. 'I'm not dark. And I don't suppose I'm good-looking.'

'No, you're not.'

'Thank you!'

'But I've known worse!'

'Thank you again.'

'I don't find you exciting.'

'I'm sorry about that.'

She laughed. 'You're getting better, Prof. I do believe you're making fun of me. I don't like men that I can walk all over.'

'I love you, Lynn. That's what I want to say. I don't care about anyone else.'

'Don't you think you should try a few more girls before you start getting ideas about marriage? And listen, Gray, you do understand, don't you? I'm not a good girl. Not at all.'

'Oh Lynn, you're talking like my Dad.'

'It's – well, I suppose I have to save you, Prof. Save you from *me*. Mind you, I'm careful. I don't let anything happen that shouldn't.'

'Lynn you *are* good. I love you. We could get a quiet place in Scotland. Just the two of us.'

'I like somewhere with a bit of life.'

'Well, perhaps we could go to Edinburgh. That's a fine city. We could get a little flat, near the centre.'

'Stop it, Graham. It won't happen. Stop it.'

'I won't stop it. And it will happen. Will, will, will. Come with me, Lynn. Think of it, just us, married. Better than Birmingham, or Jeff's café. I'll be good to you, Lynn. I'll do anything for you.'

'Oh, Graham. You're the nicest fellow I've ever met. . . .'

'I'm not *that* nice. But I'll be nice to you. Say "yes".'

'I don't know, Prof. I don't know.'

Silence. Thirty seconds. A minute.

She jumped up. 'Why not?' she cried. 'Let's go! Off to Gretna, to get married. Graham, love, I'll make you so happy. You won't believe it.'

'You were a long time,' Mrs Hollis said. 'I thought you must have gone with her.'

'She missed the nine twenty-five, and caught the ten o'clock. She'll be in Birmingham by midday.'

'Well, I must say I'm glad. And what are you going to do now, Graham? Have you done any school work? Or were you down at that awful café all week?'

'I did some work,' Graham said.

'You ought to do some more. You go back to school next week, remember?'

'The weather's too good to work in,' said Graham. 'I think I'll go for a walk in the hills.'

'It's all right for *you*, isn't it?' said his mother. 'I have got the house to clean. And all your dirty washing to do.'

Graham said nothing.

'I didn't sleep at all last night, you know. Because of you, of course. Let me tell you, Graham Hollis, I'll never forget what you did. Never.'

'Let's not talk about it, Mother,' he said. 'I'll take some food with me.'

'Well, you can get it yourself. You've got the right day for it anyway. Off you go. Don't think about me.'

'Mother, *please*!'

'You're taking plenty of food. It looks enough for an army.'

'I get hungry in the open air.'

'Well, *I* can't eat a thing. I didn't touch my breakfast.'

'I'll go upstairs and put a few things in my bag,' Graham said. 'Books maybe. I'll rest and do some of my reading in the afternoon. I won't be back till dark. And don't start worrying if I'm late.'

—You're awful, Graham Hollis. Telling all those lies!

—We must get a good start.

—They'll be worried to death tonight.

—They'll know what has happened.

—You'll break your Mother's heart, Graham Hollis.

—She can't hold me for ever. I'm going to get away now.'

—But she loves you.

—I hate her. She hid the valuables from Lynn.

—It's not right, doing this to your parents.

—I'll let them know I'm safe. When we're married.

—You don't have to marry her, boy.

—But that's what I want. Marriage. They can't touch us then. No more Jeff. Nothing like that. Just us, married.

—Hurry up, then. She'll get tired of waiting. What if she's gone?

—She won't go. She might. Wait for me, Lynn. Where's my post-office book? A hundred and ten pounds. Plenty of people marry with less. Hurry, boy, hurry. Get a few things together.... The bag's very full. Mother will wonder. No, she won't. I often go for long walks with this bag. Stay cool. Right? Right. Here I come, Lynn.

8

She was waiting in the station entrance.

'I thought . . .' he said.

'I thought . . .' she said at the same moment. They both laughed.

'You haven't changed your mind, have you, Lynn?'

'Of course I have. I've changed it lots of times. And I might change it again in a minute. So be careful!'

'Oh, don't Lynn. You won't, will you?'

'Stop worrying. I've decided. We're in business. But perhaps *you* don't really want to go. This is your last chance to go home. I won't say anything. I'm not leading you on, Prof. You're leading me on.'

'I'm not leading you on,' he said. 'We're going to get married, Lynn. M.A.R.R.I.E.D. And we'll live happily ever after.'

He put his arms round her. She blew warm breath into his ear.

'Mmmmh,' he said.

She was pressing herself against him. 'Hey, you're not a boy. You're a man,' she said. 'Hey, Prof, I want to tell you something. Listen carefully. I love you, Graham. I love you more than anyone. Except a little dog that I once had. He was called Butch. He died.'

'Thank you!'

'Of course, he was only a dog. You're a person, that's different. But you know what I mean. He didn't want anything from me. He just loved me and I loved him.'

'And *we* love *us*.' He was kissing her.

'Come on, Prof. If we're going, it's time we started,' Lynn said. 'Bonnie Scotland, here we come! Which train will we catch?'

'I don't think we should go by train,' said Graham. 'Let's go by road instead.'

'Oh, *sure*,' she said. 'Where did you park the car?'

'I mean it. We can hitch-hike. In a few hours' time people are going to come here. They'll ask questions. We've been here a long time and we've probably been noticed. So we'll let them think we've gone to London. We'll go the inquiry office and ask about the London trains. And talk and laugh a lot. Then we'll walk quietly away. You can go out by the side entrance into Mill Street. And I'll go the other way into Town Square.'

'When did you think of all this, Gray?'

'Just now, on the way to my house and back. Then we can get different buses along the Liverpool Road, as far as Scannell. And then we can meet up and start hitching. We'll be in Scotland tonight!'

'Gray, you're wonderful! Come on, let's go. The road to Gretna Green!'

'You make me feel like Young Lochinvar!'

'Young who?'

'Lochinvar. He was somebody in a book who ran off with a beautiful girl. And married her. Just like us.'

'Oh.'

'He threw her across his horse and rode off.'

'We wouldn't get far on a horse,' Lynn said. She laughed. 'But you have lovely romantic ideas, haven't you? ... now, now, that'll do. We can't stay here wasting time.'

'Oh, yes, we can,' Graham said. 'That's part of the plan. You've got to give me a nice long kiss. So that the porter over there remembers us. And then we'll go and kiss in the station café. And then at the bookshop....'

'You learn fast, don't you, Prof?' Lynn said.

Lynn got off the bus at Scannell. She was late. Graham was looking worried. 'What happened?' he cried. 'I thought you might have changed your mind again!'

'No, Prof, don't worry. I'm here now. I saw a shirt I liked in a shop window. It was only two pounds, so I bought it. I can't wait to try it on.'

'And I can't wait to start hitching! Let's go.'

'OK, love, but what time is it?'

'Half-past twelve.'

'I thought it was later than that. I'm hungry.'

'I'm not surprised. You only had a cup of tea for breakfast. Shall we have a picnic before we start?'

'That's a good idea,' said Lynn. 'Let's sit behind this wall. It'll be nice and warm in the sun.'

Graham brought out some food and drink. They began to eat bread and tomatoes. Then they ate a banana together, one at each end, until their lips met in the middle.

Lynn lay back in the sun. 'This is great,' she said. 'I wonder how Jeff's getting on.'

'Don't think about Jeff,' Graham said.

She sat up. 'I'm going to try that shirt on.'

'What, now?'

'Why not? Close your eyes.'

He closed his eyes.

'You're looking.'

'I'm not.'

'Yes, you are.'

'I'm not. I promise.'

'Well, why aren't you, then? Hey, Prof, you *are* slow.'

He opened his eyes. She was pulling the shirt straight.

'There. Do you like it?'

'Yes. It's lovely. It shows your . . . shape, doesn't it?'

'Of course it does. But you need to have a *shape* to show . . oh, Prof, I love the way you go red.'

'I wish I didn't.'

'You'll grow out of it. I think I'll keep this on. It might help us hitching.'

'Lynn, it's lovely, you're lovely.'

'Now then, Gray. You're always saying we should be moving on.'

They climbed the low stone wall and were back at the road-side.

'This could take a long time,' said Lynn. But after only two or three minutes a lorry stopped.

'Hi, Lynn,' a voice said. 'Are you going my way?'

'Good God! That's Charlie Booth. What a surprise!'

'Who's he?'

'A customer. He comes into the café sometimes.'

'What do we do now, Lynn?'

'We climb in,' she said. 'There's nothing else *to* do!'

They got in the front of the lorry. They sat side by side, pressed together. There wasn't much space.

'Where are you going, Lynn?' Charlie asked. He was a small, thin, round-faced man in early middle age.

'To the motorway.'

'You're in luck. I'll drop you at the crossroads.'

Charlie sang an old pop-song quietly. The lorry began to go faster.

'Your day off, Lynn, is it?' he said after a while.

'Well . . .'

'I've seen your friend before. He was helping in the café the other night. That's right isn't it, son?'

'Yes.'

'You won't remember me. But I remember you. I've got a good memory for faces.'

'Well, now you can start forgetting, Charlie,' said Lynn. 'Forget you've seen us. OK?'

'What are you doing, Lynn?'

'Never you mind.'

For a minute or two Charlie sang quietly and said nothing. Then, 'I don't understand you, Lynn. I don't understand.'

'You're not supposed to understand.'

'Then why do I have to keep quiet?'

'Listen, Charlie,' she said. 'I've left the job. Jeff won't like it, and I don't want him to know where I've gone. Is that enough for you?'

'I suppose so,' said Charlie. 'And what about the lad?'

'What about him?'

'He's the new boy friend, eh? He's a bit young for you, isn't he?'

'He's over eighteen.'

'He doesn't look it to me.'

'Charlie, will you just forget you've seen us?'

'OK then,' Charlie said. 'I don't owe Jeff Wright anything and I won't tell him anything. Where are you going after you get to the motorway?'

'Does it matter, Charlie?'

'I'm just interested. Don't tell me if you don't want to.'

'We're going south. Going to London.'

'Have a good time then.'

'We will.'

'Hey, Lynn,' said Charlie, 'have you heard the joke about the Englishman, the Irishman, and the Scotsman?'

'No, Charlie. Tell me.'

'Well, there were these three fellows, see. They were looking for a meal ...'

'It stops him asking questions, anyway,' breathed Lynn in Graham's ear.

'Will he really not tell Jeff?'

'Oh, I think so. Charlie's all right. It doesn't matter anyway. The main thing is to get away from Crimley.'

'Lynn! You're not listening!' said Charlie.

'I am listening, Charlie, love,' said Lynn. 'Go on.'

'So the Scotsman says "I'm not spending my money. I've brought my own!" ...'

Lynn laughed.

'That's not the end,' said Charlie. 'That's only the middle.'

'All right, Charlie. Go on. Tell us the whole joke!'

9

'Hot, isn't it?' Graham said. 'For September, I mean.'

'It's a lovely day, Prof. We chose a good one.'

'Why doesn't someone stop for us?'

'I told you, Gray. It sometimes takes a long time. Lots of drivers don't like stopping just before a motorway. And you can't hitch on a motorway. So we'll have to stay here. Someone will pick us up sooner or later. Hey, Prof, are you all right?'

'I'm fine.'

'You look ill. Are you *sure* you're all right?'

'Well . . . I do feel a bit sick. It's my head.'

'Poor Prof, is it bad?'

'It's nothing really.'

'Why don't you sit over there in the shade? And let me do the hitching. I might get better results.'

—It's not really happening.

—It *is*.

—I'm sitting behind a great big motorway sign. On the grass. In this heat. It can't be happening.

—There's still time to go home. You could easily hitch back to Crimley. They won't know that you went anywhere.

—And leave her? Back out on her now?

—She'll understand. 'OK Prof,' she'll say. 'If that's how you feel. Run along home. Don't worry about me.'

—Well, what are you waiting for? Go home while you've got the chance.

—And leave Lynn? Oh no. It's *because* she'll understand. That's why I won't leave her. Ever.

—You're not the first, you know. Or the second.

—I don't care.

52

—And you won't be the last!

—I might be. I will be. We'll get married, that's different. She said she loved me. She hasn't said that to anyone before.

—Her legs are too thick.

—I don't love her for her legs. She's good ... somebody's stopping. He's leaning out of the window she's smiling at him. I think we're off again.

'Come on, Gray. We've got a ride at last. But you'll have to sit in the back of the lorry. The driver didn't want you at all. He thought I was alone.'

'I don't mind where I sit, Lynn. I'm just happy that we're moving again.'

—It's not easy getting into the back of a lorry. Even if you're tall, like me. One leg in, that's something. Oh, hell, he's moving off. He doesn't care if I fall into the road. Hold on. Hold on, boy. Ah, that's better. Well, there's plenty of space inside. Going north at last. The road to Scotland.

—You can't turn back now.

—All right, I've done it. No, *we've* done it. We're going together.

—Your parents will miss you soon.

—My head is going round and round. It's warm in here. And dark. It's been a long tiring week. We're on the road now. I could fall asleep. I won't. No sleep. No sleep. Sleep ...

'Wake up, wake up. Rise and shine!'

'Uh?' Graham half-opened his eyes.

'Wake up, love, we've arrived.'

'Uhmmmm. What time is it, Lynn?'

'Nearly eight.'

'At night?'

'Of course it's night. You've been asleep, love. You looked sweet. But we've got to get out now.'

'Where are we?'

'Pool-on-Sea.'

'Where?'

'Pool-on-Sea.'

'That's not on the way to Scotland!'

'It's nearer to Scotland than Crimley. I think it is anyway!'

'I suppose it is,' said Graham. 'A bit nearer. But why Pool-on-Sea?'

'Because that's where Bill works.'

'Bill?'

'The man who gave us a ride. Hey, Bill, come and meet Graham.'

'How do you do, son,' said Bill. He was a tall man. As tall as Graham and nearly as thin. 'Sorry you couldn't ride in the front. But I've been hearing all about you. You're a lucky man.'

'Oh, stop it, Bill,' Lynn said. She gave him a friendly push.

Graham got down from the lorry. 'You two know each other, then?' he said.

'No,' said Lynn.

'Yes,' said Bill.

'Well, he *says* he's talked to me in the café,' said Lynn. 'But I don't believe him. You'll say anything, won't you, Bill? I know your type.'

Bill gave a broad smile.

'Now you run along, back to your wife. And thanks for the ride,' said Lynn.

'Cheerio, son,' Bill said. 'Keep an eye on her.' He got in the lorry and drove off.

'There Graham,' said Lynn. 'How are you? How's your head?'

'A bit better, I think,' said Graham. 'But Lynn, *why* did you take a ride to Pool-on-Sea?'

'I wanted to leave that horrible road. And I haven't been to Pool-on-Sea for years. There are lots of places to stay here. No one will ask any questions. We'll never be found.'

'My aunt and uncle live at Pool-on-Sea,' Graham said. 'I nearly came here for a holiday last week.'

'Lucky boy! Why didn't you?'

'I didn't want to come. And I'm glad I didn't. I met you instead.'

'And look what's happened to you. You've run off to get married. To a girl you've only known for a week!'

'I *want* to get married, Lynn. You will marry me?'

'Of course I'll marry you. Again and again if you like! But start enjoying yourself. I don't like you with that long face, Prof. . . . What are all those lights over there?'

'The fun-fair.'

'Well, what are we waiting for. Let's go and have a good time. Hungry, love?'

'I – no, Lynn. I don't think I am. Not yet. Not very.'

'I am. I could eat a horse. Here's a hot-dog stand. Two hot-dogs and two Cokes please. I could eat Young What's-his-name's horse!'

'Young Lochinvar.'

'And his girl friend? What was her name?'

'I'm not sure. Oh, yes, I remember. Ellen.'

'It sounds a bit like Lynn.'

'I suppose it does. But Graham isn't much like Lochinvar.'

'No. But you both had the same idea.'

'You know what, Lynn? You haven't told me your surname.'

'Smith.'

'What?'

'I said Smith. Here, love, are you going to eat that hot-dog or aren't you?'

'I don't feel like it.'

'Let me finish it. Are you sure you're all right, Gray?'

'Yes. Of course I am.'

'What shall we go on first? The Mountain Ride? The Sky-Wheel?'

'I don't mind, Lynn.'

'Oh, look, funny hats! Shall I get a funny hat? Which do you like best? The one that says "Boy Wanted" or "Kiss Me Slowly"? Well, I've already got a boy, haven't I? And you can kiss me slowly any time, can't you? But not now.'

—It's dark now. There are lights, coloured lights, millions of lights everywhere. There's music everywhere too. And people, people, people, people.

—It's 20p a time for the rides. . . . Oh, well, here goes.

—Mountain Ride. Up, up, up, up. Round, round, slowly, slowly: I can see all the lights and the moon's coming up, shining on the sea, on the houses, on the fair ground, round, round –

down! Hold on, all cry out. Up, round, down, up, down, down. Up, round, do-ow-ow-own, rou-ou-ou-ound. Finished.

—Star-racer. Coloured lights. Put in seat. Go round and round. Turning, turning. Pulled this way. Pushed that way. Round, round, this is hell, they love it. It's hell. Feel light-headed, round, push, pull, round, push, pull, round, push, pull round, push pull over finished.

—Sky wheel. Must we go, yes we must. Got to keep up, she's enjoying it. She hasn't noticed . . .

'Are you *sure* you're all right, love?'

'Yes, Lynn, of course. This is fun, isn't it?'

'You look white, Graham. Dead white. How's your head?'

'Not so bad.'

'You should have a rest. I ought to have noticed you're not well.'

'I *am* well.'

'Let's get some fish and chips. We can eat them sitting down.'

'I'm still not hungry, Lynn.'

'You're not feeling sick are you, Gray?'

'No.'

'We won't go on any more big rides. Let's stay on the gentle ones.'

—Tunnel of love. A quiet ride. Well, *quieter* anyway. Music. Quick kiss from Lynn. She's laughing. I still feel a bit sick.

—Fun-house. Lots of machines. Put pennies in, get nothing out. Electric games. Reach a million points and get your money back. Oh no, Lynn, not another hot dog. Not for me, Lynn, no, no, no.

—Hall of Mirrors. Walk into it. Lose each other at once. Walls of glass. Walls you can walk through. Lynn, Lynn, are you still in here? Don't be silly. Of course she's still here. Where? Can't see her. Oh, there you are, Lynn. Yes, I know I'm silly. I can't help it.

—Football game. Crowd of lads kicking real footballs. Trying to hit stand-up photographs of well-known players. Sit down, Graham boy, this is bad. Are you going to be sick? No. The lads want Lynn to have a go. She won't. Yes, she will, of course she will. Doesn't know how to kick a ball. Missed. Missed again. Oh! The smallest picture goes down. She wins a little rubber dog. Talking, laughing with all the boys. Six boys and a girl, Oh, she's having a great time. *Her* head's all right. *She* doesn't feel sick.

'Graham, sweetheart! You're ill. You ought to be in bed.'

'I'm not so bad. I feel a little better now. Go on, Lynn, enjoy yourself.'

'No, love. I'm sorry. I knew you weren't well. I should have stayed with you. All right, fellows, thanks, that was fun. Look, Gray. I won a little dog. Nice, isn't he? Just rest for a few minutes. We're not going anywhere.'

'What are we going to do, then? It's half-past ten.'

'We'll find a place to stay. The summer's nearly over. There'll be lots of empty rooms. I'll get my wedding ring out of my bag.'

'Your wedding ring?'

'Yes. Haven't you ever heard of a wedding ring?'

'But why have you got one? Lynn, you're not married, are you?'

'Of course I'm not married!'

'Then why have you got a wedding ring?'

'Oh Graham, I'll go red in a minute. I've got a wedding ring because I bought one. 50p in the market, if you must know.'

'But why . . .?

'Because a wedding ring can be a great help sometimes. Like now.'

'But, Lynn . . .'

'Because you need to be looked after, love. Because you look like death warmed up. I've got to put you to bed. We'll find some little place to stay. The sooner you're off your feet, the better. I told you my name's Smith. You can be Mr Smith, right?'

'No, it doesn't seem right, Lynn. I want to marry you, nothing less.'

'First things first, Prof. What you need is somewhere nice and warm.'

'Yes, Lynn.'

'And you need it, quickly, don't you?'

'Well – yes, Lynn.'

'Right. Well, here we are. The Rochester Hotel. It sounds better than it looks. But it'll do.'

—You're going to be sick.

—No. Hold it down. No.

—Yes.

—No. No. Not in front of her. Wait till she's out of the room.

—Yes. Get to the bathroom quickly.

—No. Oh God, no. No, no, no. Yes.

'Sorry, Lynn. Oh, I'm sorry.'

'Don't worry, love. I knew it was coming. I'm glad we got here in time. It was bad, wasn't it? You're shaking.'

'I'm all right now.'

'Poor old Prof. It doesn't worry me. I just feel sorry for you. You don't look very happy. Here, let's get you into bed. Nice and warm, that's what you need . . . you *are* thin, aren't you?'

'I suppose so, Lynn. I can't help it.'

'Still, it's better than being fat.'

'Lynn.'

'What is it, Gray?'

'When we get married I'll get you a *real* wedding ring. Made of gold. To keep for ever.'

'That'll be lovely.'

'Because we'll be married for the rest of our lives. You want that, don't you Lynn?'

'Yes, love. I thought we were a bit silly to come. And maybe we were. But I'm glad we did.'

'Oh, Lynn, Lynn, Lynn.'

'You're feeling better, aren't you, Gray?'

'I'm feeling much better. And I'm not sleepy.'

'Aren't you? Well, I am. So just lie quiet.'

'Yes, Lynn.'

'We've got plenty of time.'

'Yes, Lynn. The rest of our lives.'

'That's right, love. Let's hope so, anyway. Goodnight, Prof, love. God bless.'

—Coming up, slowly, slowly. Don't want to wake, must wake. Wake up, wake up.

—Lynn's lying there. She's asleep. Dead to the world. She's breathing gently, like a cat.

—Hey! Graham Hollis! You've left home! With her!

—I know. I must be mad.

—They'll be looking for you. They'll know by now. They were up all night. Ringing the police every half hour.

—Oh, God. Yes.

—They'll be hunting now. The police, with their two-way radios. Missing from home in Crimley, Graham Hollis, sixteen, tall, thin, fair. Probably travelling with a blonde girl. . . .

—Come on, boy. You're not that important. There won't be a nationwide search. You're not a child missing from school.

—They'll describe you. They'll tell the police everywhere.

—Will they? I don't know what they do.

—They're hunting for you. You're hunted, wanted. Hunted. Wanted.

—They don't know where to look. They'll ask at Crimley Station. We'll be remembered there. We were there for an hour. Asking about London. That's where young people go. London. They won't think of Pool-on-Sea. We were clever.

—What about Charlie? In the lorry.

—He doesn't know much. And why should he care?

—Go back, boy! Go back!

—I can't. It's too late.

—Yes, you can. Just get an early train. It was only a little adventure, soon forgotten. It's over now. Nothing ever happened.

—What do you mean, nothing happened?

—You know. Nothing *has* happened. Yet. Get out while you can.

—I can't. I won't. I love her. *Love* her.

—You're a missing person. Hunted.

—They won't look for us here.

—Hunted. What about Uncle Roger and Aunt Josie, a few streets away? Get home quick. Or else.

—Or else? Cool down, cool down. Or else what? Or else continue as planned. Go to Scotland. Live there for a week or two. Get married. And then we're safe. Safe, married, in love for ever. ... We ought to be on our way. What is the time? Nearly nine o'clock! It's later than I thought. I'm hungry. I feel all right now. I'll get some breakfast. Eight till nine, the notice said, I'll wake her up. Gently, gently. Just a touch. No effect. Kiss her awake. Go on, don't be afraid. Kiss her ... she's a good sleeper.

Her hand moved across her face and pushed him away. 'What is it? What's up?'

'Morning, Lynn.'

'Go to hell!' She turned over and pulled up the bed-clothes.

'Lynn! Time for breakfast.'

'I don't *eat* breakfast!'

'Well, I'll go, Lynn, if you don't mind. I'm hungry after yesterday.'

'Don't talk about it. Do it.'

Graham dressed. As he went out she said, 'Bring me some tea.'

'I'll ring for some if you like, Lynn.'

'Ring for it? in a place like this? Don't be silly. Bring a cup back with you.'

She put her head out from under the bed-clothes. 'Did you bring me that cup of tea?'

'They didn't let me.'

'They didn't what?'

'I asked the woman. She said you can't take tea-cups into the bedrooms.'

61

'Well, you silly — oh, forget it. You don't *ask*. You just *take* it while nobody's looking.'

'Sorry, Lynn. Is there anything else I can do?'

'Yes. You can go and get me some cigarettes. Go on. Don't start kissing me now. I don't feel like it.'

—God, what a day. Cold and wet. Wind blowing in from the sea. Some people are still on holiday. In weather like this!

—Cigarettes. Where can I get some cigarettes? Not in this street. There's nothing here but cheap hotels. I'll try the newspaper shop on the sea front.

—Look out! A policeman.

—So what, a policeman?

—I'm a missing person. Hunted.

—Don't be so silly. He doesn't know who you are.

—Missing boy aged sixteen, tall . . .

—One person in 50 million. There's nothing to worry about.

—Why's your heart beating so fast, then?

—I must stop worrying. We'll soon be in Scotland, safe and married.

—Married? You saw her this morning. Do you want *that* every day?

—Plenty of people are awful when they wake up.

—She uses bad language.

—I love her.

—She's *not* a nice girl.

—I love her.

—The newspaper shop's open, anyway.

'Ten cigarettes please. . . . Thank you.'

'Hey, son, what about your change?'

'Oh, thank you, I forgot.'

—Careful. They'll notice you.

—Don't be silly. People forget their change every day. And in this wind and rain nobody notices anything. It's not a day for walking. Some people *are* walking along the sea front, though. Like that man over there with the dog. It looks a bit like Uncle Roger's dog, Sandy.

—Sandy! That *is* Sandy!

—I don't think so. He's a long way off. It's just another dog.

—And the man coming up behind. It's Uncle Roger!

—I can't *see* from here.

—It is him! And look, he's calling!

—Turn round! Into the side-street, quick! Nowhere to hide. Run along, right to the end. A doorway at last ... he's going past.

—He looked this way.

—He didn't.

—He did. It was Uncle Roger.

—Rubbish! It was just a man with a dog. Come on, boy. Take it easy. Cool down. Walk slowly back to the hotel. Breathe deeply, all's well.

—What if it *was* him, though? What if he tells the police?

'Hullo, Gray.'

'Hullo, Lynn. I brought your cigarettes. Lynn, listen. I think we—'

'Thank you, Prof. You're a love. I'm sorry I bit your head off. I'm like that in the morning. I can't help it.'

'It doesn't matter, Lynn. I think we should leave.'

'OK, love. No hurry. Sit down and talk to me.'

'I thought I saw my Uncle Roger.'

'Did you? Gray, love, your clothes are wet. Take them off.'

'My Uncle Roger. He was walking on the sea front with his dog.'

'Was he, now?'

'Yes, Lynn. And I thought he saw me.'

'Forget what *he* saw, love. *You* look at me. Am I nice?'

'Oh, Lynn, yes. You're lovely. But what I'm trying to say is this. If my Uncle saw me, he'll telephone my parents. Or tell the police. So I think we ought to leave.'

'Did he follow you?'

'No, but ...'

'Then stop worrying. I want you to be happy. You can't start too soon.'

63

'But Lynn . . .'

'There, you must come to me. And take it easy. I love you, Gray. I've never said that to a fellow before. I really love you. I'm going to show you that I love you.'

'Lynn, no. We've got to go *now*.'

'Gray. Yes.'

'No. Not yet.'

'Oh, come on Prof. Are you a man or a mouse? I don't do this for everyone, I can tell you!'

'I know, Lynn. But don't you see? I just want us to be married. To have all our lives together.'

'There's something about you, Prof, that's not natural.'

'Lynn that's not true. I do love you, I do want you. But I want to get away from Pool-on-Sea. Will you come? Please?'

'Oh, go to hell.'

'We could get to Edinburgh today, Lynn. We could go by train. Change at Cobchester. I've still got nearly all my money. I don't mind spending it.'

'I've never been to Scotland. I'm not sure I want to go.'

'But Lynn, that was the whole idea. You said you loved me, only five minutes ago.'

'Five minutes ago is five minutes ago. Listen, Prof. I only came with you because I was angry with Jeff. And listen again. If I get married, I'll marry a *real* man. Someone with blood in him, not milk and water.'

'Lynn, I do . . .'

'Just look at me. Sitting here in my nightdress, arguing. That *is* fun, isn't it! You run off home to your mummy and daddy, and don't waste any more of my time.'

'All right, if that's how you feel.'

'It *is* how I feel.'

'And what will you do, Lynn?'

'What's it got to do with you?'

'Don't go back to Crimley.'

'I will if I want. And I won't if I don't want. Are you afraid I'll say hello to you in the street when you're with your parents?'

'I wasn't thinking of that.'

'Do you want me to give you a note to take home. Dear Mr

and Mrs Hollis. Your son is still a little boy. Keep him away from grown-up girls!'

'Oh Lynn, don't. And don't send me away, please.'

'Don't cry on me, son. Go on, get out before I get dressed. I'm not putting on a show for you.'

'I won't go back to my parents.'

'You will.'

'No, I won't. I don't know what I'll do. I'll kill myself first.'

'You know very well you won't.'

'I'll do *something*. I'll never go back to Crimley. It's the end of everything that matters. I won't have anything to care about.'

'Here, take this, then, you big baby!' She threw the rubber dog at him.

'Lynn!'

'What, you again? Haven't you gone yet?'

'Lynn. I'm sorry. I *was* a baby.'

'Did you come back to tell me that?'

'I'm learning my lesson. I'm going to grow up.'

'That's interesting. When? This year? Next year?'

'As quickly as I can. Starting today. Lynn, have I really lost you?'

'You never had me.'

'I mean, is this really the end?'

'I told you, go home and be good.'

'I won't go back, Lynn. I'll find a job and grow up by working. And — well if we're finished, all I can do is wish you well.'

He put out his hand.

Then she had her arms round him. She was laughing, laughing.

'What are you laughing at?'

'Oh, Prof,'

'I don't see what's funny about it.'

'Don't you? I do. Graham, love, I'm glad you came back. You're so lovely sometimes. I should have known better. You don't understand women, love. I suppose you've got a lot to learn. Still, you'll learn plenty before we've finished!'

'We'll never finish, Lynn. Never.'

'All right, love. Have you started growing up already?'

'You're laughing at me again.'

'I'm not, really. Now, what about your Uncle. Are you *sure* it was him?'

'No, Lynn, I'm not sure. He might not know I've left home, anyway. But I don't feel right. We're too near home and the people who know us. I want to be a long way away.'

'In Scotland, eh?'

'Yes.'

'Then let's do it right, Gray. Have they got a phone here? Ring for a taxi to the station. Gray . . .'

'Yes, Lynn.'

'It's a long way to Edinburgh.'

'Yes, it is Lynn. We don't have to stay there. But we do have to go to Scotland to get married.'

'I know, Gray. But we don't have to do it all at once, do we? We have to change trains at Cobchester, you said. I've got a girl friend in Cobchester. Her name's Betty. She's married. I want to see her again. They've got a flat. There's only the two of them and the baby. We could stay there, love.'

'How long for?'

'Just for a night or two. And then go on to Edinburgh on Monday. We can't get married before Monday, can we?'

'I suppose not. But . . .'

'We'll be safe in Cobchester. Nobody will know us there.'

'No, but . . .'

'Have you got a better idea?'

'No, but . . .'

'Leave it to me, then. We'll be all right. Just get two one-way tickets to Cobchester.'

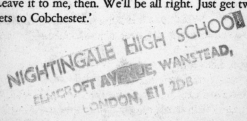

11

'Ring the bell again, Gray.'

'It's no good, Lynn. Nobody's coming.'

'It's Saturday. Betty has probably gone shopping. We'll go for a cup of tea and come back later. Oh, wait a minute, Gray, I can hear footsteps. There *is* somebody at home. Here they come. Hullo, Tim. How are you? This is Graham Hollis, a friend of mine.'

'What do you want?'

'I came to see Betty, that's all.'

'She's not here.'

'When'll she be back, Tim?'

'What do you want her for?'

'We're old friends, Tim, you know that. We played together when we were kids. That was before I went to Birmingham, when we both lived round the corner in Orchid Grove. Of course, it's changed a lot now.'

'I said what do you want?'

'Well, we thought we might stay with you for a night or two. If that's all right. And then we'll move on.'

'You can move on right now!'

'It's not for long, Tim. We're travelling on business. To London or Scotland or somewhere.'

'I said no!'

'We're not just trying to save a pound or two. I wanted to see Betty. I haven't seen her for over a year. You were only just married.'

'I told you, Betty's not here.'

A voice came from behind him. 'Who is it, Tim?'

Tim called without turning round. 'Nobody.'

'Betty!' Lynn cried. 'It's me, Lynn!'

Tim stepped forward, and closed the door behind him. He

was a large man with a heavy face. 'For the last time, Lynn,' he said. 'You're not seeing her. Go away. *And* your friend.' He moved forward. 'Quick!'

Lynn looked up at the sky, as if for help. 'Come on, Gray,' she said. 'We're not staying where we're not wanted.'

Graham followed her down the stairs.

'I didn't like turning my back on him,' he said. 'I thought he was going to kick us from behind.'

'Yes. And he might have done, too. Sorry, love. ... That's marriage for you.'

'What do you mean, Lynn?'

'She married him, you see? And what can you do then? She's got a baby, and another coming, and now she's a prisoner. She's signed her life away. I've seen it happen before.'

'But not often, Lynn. Not these days.'

'Don't you believe it, Prof. Fellows who want to please you *before* they get married – they change afterwards. They get the power and then they use it. And if you've got a baby, or two or three, you can't do anything about it. You don't know *anything*, Prof. You don't know what life's about. You don't know that you're born!'

'That doesn't sound like our world, Lynn.'

'Perhaps it doesn't sound like yours. It sounds like mine. Maybe it's more like your world than you think. Old Mother Nature's the same as she always was. There's only one way round her – and that's not to have babies. That's why I'm careful.'

'Lynn, Lynn, darling. You don't think I'll make you a prisoner, do you?'

'No, love, of course I don't.'

'I'll play fair with you, Lynn. Always.'

'Always is a long time, Gray.'

'Don't you believe me?'

'There, there. Am I hurting your feelings again? I believe you, Gray. You're kind. You've got a heart. You'll be lovely to the girl you marry.'

'Which is you. And we're going to be happy ever after. Look, Lynn, it's stopped raining and the sun's coming out. We're together and everything's lovely and I love you.'

'Thanks, Prof. I'm all right now. I was feeling a bit low, thinking about Betty. We were children together round here. These flats are new. They pulled all the old houses down. Do you see that water? That's the river. And those small houses on the edge of it, by the old bridge? I remember those. That's all that is left of the old place.'

'We ought to be going, Lynn. Back to the station to get a train north.'

'It's getting a bit late, Prof. It's past four o'clock.'

'You want to stay in Cobchester tonight don't you, Lynn? You're still not quite sure about Edinburgh.'

'That's right, Prof. You *are* learning about me, aren't you. I didn't think you understood.'

'I can understand just a little bit, Lynn. Perhaps because it's somebody I love.'

'Well, all right. . . . I'm still thinking of that place down by the old bridge, Gray. We played there when we were young. There was a room at the top of one of those houses. We played there for hours. . . . Here, Gray, I've just had an idea. Come over and have a look.'

They crossed a rough space to the small houses next to the river.

'It all seems a bit sad, doesn't it,' Graham said. 'All empty and broken-down. Even in this sunshine.'

'Yes. But now, come round this side. Do you see that door up there? That's where we played houses. We can climb up the fire-escape.'

'What are we going to do?'

'You go first. Then try and open the window. I'm really surprised the window isn't broken. That's right, Gray, up you go. Now, push the window up, if it still moves. Great, you're in. What's it like in there?'

Graham put his head out of the window. 'Not bad,' he said. 'It's dry.'

'It always was dry. It's got a good roof.' Lynn climbed the metal steps and stood beside Graham.

They were in a long room, high in the middle and low at the sides. Light came in through three dirty windows. There was an old bed and some grey blankets. There were two or three pieces of broken furniture and a wooden table. Dust was everywhere.

'Well,' said Lynn. 'I don't know about you love, but I've slept in worse places than this. Much worse.'

'Lynn, you weren't thinking . . .?'

'Of course I was, love. And I still am. It's just the place for a quiet weekend.'

'Hullo, Lynn. Here I am.'

'Hullo, Gray, love. You were a long time, weren't you?'

'I had to wait at the fish and chip shop. They were making some fresh chips.'

'You've brought lots, love. That's good. I'm hungry.'

'Lynn, you've cleaned the place, haven't you?'

'Well, I suppose so. I'm not a great one for housework and all that, so don't get the wrong idea. But I couldn't live with all that dirt. I think someone was living here until a few months ago. He left us everything we needed. There's a brush for the floor, and an old shirt that I used for dusting. And I found these plates that we're eating off and two cups. So let's have that orange drink. I'm thirsty.'

'And did he leave the radio?'

'No, that's mine. I put it in the bottom of my bag when I left Jeff's. It makes the place feel like home, doesn't it?'

'Yes, Lynn. Maybe we should turn it down. We don't want anyone to know we're here.'

'I suppose so. That's better, isn't it? I'd forgotten this place for years, but I remember now. There were a few of us who played here. Betty and I and the two Thompsons, Harold and Jean. Harold was a year or two older. He was a bright little boy. Somebody told me he went to Oxford University. It makes you think, doesn't it? Do you want some more chips, Gray?'

'I've had enough, Lynn.'

'Then I'll eat them . . . you know, Gray, young Harold didn't come from a good family. The Thompsons were really rough. But you, you've got everything. You don't want to throw it all away, do you? Not really.'

'Don't say things like that, Lynn, I know what I'm doing.'

'I hope you do, love. Mmm. Those fish and chips were good. I feel nice and comfortable now. .... Are you warm enough, Gray?'

'I'm just right. But I've been wondering if you were warm enough, like that.'

'Oh, so you did notice, then?'

'It's very difficult *not* to notice, Lynn. You changed while I was out. You're wearing your nightdress under your coat.'

'You noticed but you didn't say anything.'

'I thought we should eat. While the food was hot.'

'That's a good boy. First things first. Graham, you're going red again.'

'I'm sorry, Lynn, I can't help it.'

'Don't say sorry, love. Tell me, do you like my nightie?'

'Yes, Lynn, very much.'

'It's pretty isn't it?'

'Yes. Very.'

'And me?'

'Oh, Lynn, yes, yes, yes.'

'You're shaking, love. That's no good. Easy now, don't think about yourself. Just be natural. This isn't one of your exams. Don't worry, Graham, you haven't a care in the world. Not at this minute, you haven't. Not a care in the world.'

'Don't keep saying sorry, love. There's no need.'

'I wasn't very good, Lynn.'

'Of course you weren't. You can't do everything right first time. You'll be all right. It'll get better and better.'

'I didn't mean it to be like this. I wanted us to be married first. You know that, don't you?'

'I know, love. You've said it often enough.'

'I didn't go off with you just for a – bit of fun.'

'What's wrong with a bit of fun?'

'Lynn, you're still wearing your wedding ring from the market.'

'So I am, love.'

'I want to buy you a real one. But until I do, will you wear this one for me?'

'What do you mean, Gray?'

'Well – look, give it to me. Let me put it on your finger. With this ring, I . . .'

'No, Gray, no!'

'Why not, Lynn?'

'No, I tell you! Don't do that!'

'Is it because I – wasn't much good?'

'It's not that, love. You've nothing to worry about. But I don't like this wedding ring business. It doesn't feel right.'

'It feels right to me.'

'Graham, you've still got a lot to learn. Now get some rest.'

'A lot has happened since we were at Pool-on-Sea. Everything's happened since then.'

'Do you feel different, Gray?'

'Not really different. But I love you even more. You were nice just now. You could have laughed at me.'

'I won't laugh at you, Gray.'

'Lynn! They'll still be looking for us!'

'They won't find us here, love. So lie down and get some sleep. Goodnight. Prof, love. God bless.'

12

'Gray.'

'Yes, Lynn.'

'Why aren't you asleep?'

'Why aren't *you*?'

'I don't know. I was just thinking.'

'What about, Lynn?'

'Oh, about us. And your Mum and Dad. What were you thinking about, Gray?'

'We're running away, Lynn. It still worries me.'

'Listen, Gray. I'm eighteen. I'm grown-up. You're nearly seventeen. We're not the first girl and boy to go missing. The police won't waste any time over us.'

'But my parents. And Jeff. Suppose Jeff is searching for you....'

'I'm not worried about Jeff. Maybe he wants me back, maybe he doesn't. But he won't leave his café to hunt for me. You don't know Jeff. Now your parents, they're different. But they don't know where to look for us. There are only two ways they could find you. One's if you go back.'

'I won't do that.'

'The other is if somebody tells them where you are.'

'But who, Lynn, who?'

'I don't know. I was only saying what *could* happen.'

'But Lynn, you've just said that nobody knows where we are. How could anybody tell them?'

'I don't know, love. I don't know.'

'I'm surprised that you thought about it.'

'Anything can happen, love. You might go back because you want to.'

'That's not nice, Lynn. I've told you I won't.'

'I know, Gray. But you're not like me. I just put things behind me and forget them. And I never cared about anybody much.

Why should I? Nobody's ever cared about *me*. But *you*, Gray, you think and you care. And before long you'll start thinking about your Mum and Dad. Anyway, now that you've spent the night with a girl, you'll want to go home again.'

'That's not nice, either.'

'Maybe I'm *not* nice. Maybe that's another thing. Maybe it's just a girl you wanted, *any* girl.'

'I could hate you for saying that.'

'I'm sorry, love. I don't want it to be true. But are you sure? Are you really sure?'

'Yes, I'm sure, Lynn. I love you. For being who you are. Not just for – you know. You believe me, Lynn, don't you? You've got to believe me.'

'All right, love. I believe you. Perhaps you know what you want, Prof. But do you know what's best for you?'

'What was that, Lynn? What did you say?'

'Nothing, love.'

'Gray.'

'Yes, Lynn.'

'You're still not asleep!'

'I'm just thinking.'

'About them.'

'Yes.'

'How'll they be taking it, Gray?'

'Badly. My Mother'll be crying a lot. Dad will be quieter. But he'll feel it just as much. I suppose I'm all they've got. Their world has come down round their ears.'

'So you go back in three weeks' time. And you'll say, "Hullo, Mum and Dad. I'm married. Here she is." Do you think that'll make them happy?'

'Well ...'

'It won't, will it?'

'Maybe not. But they won't be able to change anything.'

'Your Mum will never stop hating me. Because I took her blue-eyed boy away from her. Your Dad – well, I don't know. He'll want me to speak good English and go to a tennis club.

74

Now that's no good either, is it, Gray?'

'Here, Lynn, whose side are you on?'

'Yours, love. Look, Gray, I don't care if your parents go to hell. But you've got the rest of your life to think about. That's what's worrying me.'

'Well, stop worrying and get some sleep. I love you, Lynn.'

'OK, Prof. If that's what you say. Goodnight, Prof, love.'

'Goodnight, Lynn, love. God bless.'

—There's the sound of a church clock somewhere. And trains on the bridge. This is a hard bed! She's got the blankets. No peace.

—It's midnight. I've been here for ever. Under a roof, somewhere in Cobchester. With her. She's breathing softly like a cat. A well-fed cat.

—She's asleep anyway.

—Think of *them*. That's the heart of the matter.

—Haven't *I* any rights? Hasn't she?

—They only have you. Their world has fallen about their ears. After all these years. They've done everything for you. They love me.

—She loves me too.

—How long for? Today, tomorrow, next week? Then there'll be someone else. She's only a bit of skirt, that's all.

—No.

—You've got what you wanted.

—No, no.

—It wasn't all that wonderful, either.

—Shut up.

—You've got the rest of your life. Good home, good job. Don't let them go.

—No.

—Accountancy gives you a place in the world. Grow up. Leave her while you can.

—No.

—Sunshine through a dirty window.

'Graham!'

'Huh! What?'

'Graham. *Graham.*'

'Hullo, Lynn.'

'It's past ten o'clock, Gray. And it looks a lovely day out there. How are you feeling?'

'Not bad, Lynn. Not bad at all. How are you?'

'I'm fine. I like this place, don't you, Gray? It feels more and more like home.'

'It's because we're together . . . Anywhere's nice with you.'

'You still say the loveliest things, Gray.'

'And listen, Lynn. I've thought about everything. I know it'll hurt Mum and Dad. But we have our lives to live too. We've more life left than they have. And I decided. I'm quite sure. I'm not going back.'

'I see, love. And what if something happens to me?'

'What sort of something? What could happen?'

'Well – I might fall under a bus or something.'

'You won't fall under a bus.'

'Or – we could have an argument. I might get angry and walk out.'

'Lynn, if you walk out on me I'll follow you to the ends of the earth. Anyway, I'm not going back to Crimley. I'm free and I'm staying free.'

'That's what you feel now, Gray. You won't always feel like that.'

'Oh, yes, I will. Always. I've decided. But Lynn, please don't talk about walking out on me. Promise me you won't do anything like that.'

'Now, now, Prof, you haven't any right to ask for a promise.'

'I don't care if I have the right or not. I *am* asking for it. I'll give you the same promise, Lynn. I won't walk out on you.'

'All right, Gray. I promise. I won't walk out on you.'

'Oh, Lynn, it's wonderful to be certain. I feel ten feet tall today. I've never been so happy. Lynn, come here!'

'Don't you think we're close enough, Prof? Hey, Prof!'

'Don't call me "Prof" today, Lynn. I don't feel like "poor little Prof" any more.'

'No, I can see you don't.'

'Oh, Lynn, you're so wonderful. I love, love, love, love you. If you cut me with a knife you'll find I *have* got blood inside. Not just milk and water.'

'I believe you, love. . . . Here, I thought you were the slow one.'

'I'm learning.'

'You're learning pretty fast, aren't you, Gray? You're a bad boy. What will they think of you now?'

'I don't care what they think of me now. I only care about you.'

'Here, Gray. I'm thirsty, aren't you?'

'There's some of that orange drink left in the bottle. Coming over.'

'Mmmmm. That was good. Do you want some?'

'Yes, please, Lynn. I suppose this is our breakfast.'

'Yes, love. I never feel like eating in the morning.'

'I have a good hot breakfast usually. But today I don't mind. This is the nicest breakfast I've ever had in my life. Drinking orange out of the same bottle with you. It's the happiest day of my life.'

'Good for you, love.'

'I feel on top of the world, Lynn. Look at the sunlight moving over the wall. It'll reach *us* in a minute. And we're going to be married, Lynn. Married! ... They won't catch us, will they, Lynn. Nobody could tell them, could they?'

'Well – you can't be too sure.'

'What do you mean, Lynn? How can anyone catch us? Who *could* give us away?'

'I – oh, I don't know.'

'Don't worry me, Lynn. You gave me such funny look then.'

'There, there, Graham, darling, it was nothing. That's a strange word, isn't it, "darling"? It doesn't sound natural when I say it.'

'It sounds fine to me. Lynn, darling, Lynn, darling, Lynn, darling. I can't think of anything nicer.'

'Oh Gray, you're just like poor little Butch. He had that same look. He tried hard to be a big dog. But he was only the same little Butch. He was run over in the end. By a heavy lorry. . . . I don't want you to get hurt, Gray.'

'What do you mean, Lynn. There's only one way I can be hurt.'

'There are a hundred ways, Prof. You don't know, you're like my Butch. You're only little.'

'What do you mean, only little? I'm six foot two. How tall are you?'

'I'm five foot six.'

'Who's little, then?'

'You know what I mean, Gray. You're still a boy. I'm years older than you. Now lie down. Go on being happy for a bit.'

'I don't just want to be happy for a bit. I want to be happy all my life. Do you want me to be happy all my life, Lynn?'

'Yes, love.'

'You know what to do, then.'

'Yes, love.'

'Are you hungry?'

'Well, yes I am, Lynn.'

'I could eat that horse again!'

'I'm glad I'm not Young Lochinvar. Running away with you might cost a lot. Horses aren't cheap!'

'I want to go out for a meal.'

'Why don't we have another picnic? If we go out, we'll have to see other people.'

'I want to go somewhere nice. I do, really.'

'All right, Lynn. If that's what you want. You've got that funny look on your face again. As if you've been thinking.'

'Even *I* think sometimes! Not often, but sometimes.'

'You've been thinking something you don't want to tell me. I'm worried.'

'I'm tired of telling you, *don't worry*. Now, come on, Prof. Put some clothes on. Let's go.'

'Where shall we go?'

'You said this is the happiest day of your life. Well, let's make it a day to remember. We'll go to the Royal Britannia Hotel.'

'But Lynn, we can't. It'll cost too much.'

'I'll pay. I've got twenty pounds in my bag. The money that Jeff owed me.'

'I think we should be careful. We'll need all our money in Edinburgh. Before we get jobs.'

'We'll be careful with your money. But we'll enjoy mine. I won't take no for an answer.'

'I'm not dressed well enough. I can't go to the best hotel in town wearing this.'

'You're all right for the "Railway Room".'

'You seem to know a lot about it.'

'This is my home town, remember?'

'You came to Cobchester with Jeff, didn't you?'

'Now listen, Prof. You know all about Jeff and me. How long have you known me?'

'Nine days, Lynn.'

'I lived a long time before that. And I've done a lot that you don't know about.'

'I know, Lynn. I'm sorry I mentioned Jeff. I don't care what you've done. I'm just worried about what we're doing now.'

'There, love, I know. I'll tell you what we're doing. We're going out for a lovely meal, and I'm paying.'

'And after that, Lynn?'

'I don't know what we're doing after that.'

'Well, I'll tell you. We're coming back here and going to bed early. Then first thing tomorrow morning we're going to Scotland. All right?'

'All right, love. If you say so.'

13

'Lynn! There you are! Where have you been?'

'I told you, Graham, I went to have a wash. You weren't getting worried, were you?'

'Well – yes. I suppose I'm silly. There's something about a hotel sitting-room that worries me. I felt I could wait here all my life. Waiting and waiting for someone who doesn't come.'

'Now *that's* not nice, Prof. I promised not to walk out on you.'

'I'm sorry, Lynn. You were away for so long. I thought I saw you go out once. Another time, I thought you were telephoning.'

'What?'

'Telephoning. I walked around the entrance hall for something to do. There was someone just leaving one of the phone boxes. I thought it was you. But she had her back to me. Then she disappeared round a corner before I got there.'

'It must have been somebody else, love. I was having a wash. Here, Gray, how do I look now?'

'You look wonderful, Lynn.'

'Well, then, let's go and eat. Here, take this, Gray. It's to pay the bill.'

'It's too much, Lynn.'

'It's not, love. It won't cost much less than that. We're going to have a really good meal. And we're not going to hurry. The happiest day of your life. That's what you said. So start looking happy. You are still happy, love, aren't you?'

'Yes, Lynn.'

'Well, that's that, love. Did you enjoy the meal?'

'Yes, Lynn, thank you. Thank you very much. I must give you the change.'

'Don't be silly, Prof, I don't want it.'

'There wasn't much, anyway.'

'I told you. It costs the earth to eat at a place like this.'

'Then why . . .?'

'Let's not talk about it. Let's sit here a bit longer before we go.'

'Why, Lynn?'

'Well, it's nice and warm.'

'It's too warm, I think. And we've been here for hours. It's a fine day outside, Lynn. Why don't we walk back to our own little place by the river? And then we'll be lovely and warm, and by ourselves.'

'I want to sit here, Gray. I . . . I . . .'

'Lynn! Are you all right?'

'It's nothing love. Don't take any notice. I can't help it. I'm still thinking of poor little Butch. And I can't help crying. The world just stepped on him. He never knew what hit him.'

'Lynn, darling, don't cry. Smile. Look, I'm smiling.'

'Yes, Gray, you are, aren't you? . . . Poor little Butch.'

'Lynn! Who's that man crossing the entrance hall? That big fellow. I've seen him before.'

'Have you, love?'

'He's coming this way. Lynn! Is it somebody looking for us? Do you think we should run?'

'Take it easy, Graham. It's only Sam Bell. There's nothing wrong, you'll soon see. . . . Hullo, Sam, I'm glad you've come. Graham, here, was a bit worried. But I didn't want to tell him the good news till you came.'

'Good news?' Graham said. 'What good news, Lynn? And I *thought* I knew him. I *do* know him.'

'Of course you know me, son,' said Sam Bell. 'We met in the café. You tried to hit me. Remember?'

'I remember,' Graham said. 'But what's happening, Lynn? What's happening?'

'There, now, love. It's like this, Gray. You thought you saw me telephoning, right? Well, I suppose you did see me telephoning. I remembered that my old friend, Sam, lives in Cobchester. And he goes up to Scotland sometimes. So I thought, perhaps old Sam's going up in the next few days. He might take us up and save us a lot of trouble. So I rang him. And we're in

luck, Graham. Sam *is* going up there. This very day. And that's
the good news. We've got a ride.'

'Today's Sunday,' Graham said.

'You don't know much about lorry-driving, do you, love? Sam
goes up today, empty. He fills up the lorry tomorrow morning.
That's right, isn't it, Sam?'

'That's right, Lynn.'

'But why didn't you tell me, Lynn? We're in this together.
You can tell me anything.'

'Well, I was a bit worried about you meeting Sam again. Now
you can see him face to face, you know he's friendly.'

'It's all right, son,' said Sam. 'I've forgotten what happened.'

'I didn't know you and Lynn were such old friends.'

'We've known each other a long time. I'm always dropping
into Jeff's. But don't worry. There's never been anything between us. I'm married, you know. Still, I'm jealous of you in a
way. . . .'

'He knows about us, Gray.'

'I can see that. Where does Jeff come into this,' Graham
asked.

'He doesn't. Jeff's no friend of mine. If I can help you I will.
Do you believe me, son?'

'I suppose so.'

'You don't sound too sure. Here, Lynn, you tell him. You
know I mean well, don't you?'

'Yes,' said Lynn, very quietly.

'I've got my lorry parked in a side street. The doorman didn't
want it in front of the hotel.'

'Bring it round, Sam. We'll see you in a minute. . . . There you
are, Gray, everything's planned. We'll drive off from the Royal
Britannia Hotel in a lorry!'

'Lynn. Do you believe him? Really?'

'Sam and I understand each other,' said Lynn.

'So it's goodbye to the old home,' Graham said.

'Yes, love.'

'We've only been here since yesterday. But I feel sad leaving

82

it. We were happy last night and this morning. Weren't we, Lynn?'

'Yes, love. But you wanted to move on, didn't you? Where's Sam? Hey, Sam! We're up here in the last house.'

Sam stood in the long, low room. 'That table doesn't look bad,' he said. 'The wood's still good. My wife's been looking for a nice kitchen table. How can we get it out of here?'

'You don't want that old thing, Sam,' said Lynn.

'Of course I do. Now what came in must go out, eh? There must be a way.'

'It'll go through the door at the end. Somebody outside could help it down. But you're wasting your time,' said Lynn.

'I don't think so. And there's plenty of room in the back of the lorry. Here, son. You'll help me, won't you?'

Graham said nothing.

'Those chairs look all right too,' said Sam. 'You don't get much for nothing these days. And that piece of carpet. There's nothing wrong with that either. Come on, son, I'm helping you, so you can help me. It won't take five minutes to take this lot.'

'Don't look like that, Prof,' said Lynn. 'Sam's got a house. He needs furniture. He's glad to get all he can.'

'We're all glad of what we can get, aren't we?' said Sam.

'Look, Prof, we're going up in the world. How far are we from Scotland, Sam?'

'About an hour's drive at this speed.'

'An hour. That's not long, is it? Is it Prof?'

'We'll be there before it gets dark, then,' Graham said.

'And we're not going very fast, either,' said Lynn. 'Young "What's-his-hame" could go nearly as fast on his horse. Don't you think so, Prof?'

'I suppose so, Lynn.'

'But we're not on a horse. We're in the front of Sam's lorry. It's not quite the same ... you're not saying much, Prof. Are you tired?'

'A bit.'

'This is supposed to be the exciting part.'

'I feel strange, Lynn. Nothing seems real. I seem to be in a dream. The kind of dream that goes on and on, and you never reach where you are going. I'm glad I'm not in a dream . . . Lynn, you're crying again. Are you still thinking of Butch?'

'Sorry, love. It came over me again suddenly. I'm better now. Here, Gray, tell me some more about Young "What's-his-name." '

'Oh there's a lot of it, Lynn. We read about it at school. He was a famous soldier. He fell in love and rode off with the fair Ellen. And he was followed by her parents. They tried to catch him . . . Lynn! You've still got tears in your eyes. You're not crying for Young Lochinvar, are you? They didn't stop him. He got his girl . . . Hey, Mr Bell. Is something the matter?'

'It's nothing much, son. The lorry's having trouble with this hill. I just want to look at the engine. I'll stop in this parking space here. You two can have a little walk.'

'I ought to help him, Lynn.'

'He'll ask you if he needs help, love. Sam knows all about engines.'

'It's taking him a long time.'

'Don't *worry* so. It doesn't matter.'

'It's getting dark, Lynn. I can just see those hills over there. Do you think they're in Scotland?'

'Maybe they are, love.'

'I wish we were there and married.'

'Gray. Here. I want to kiss you.'

'That was nice, Lynn.'

'I do love you, Gray. You'll always be "Young Lochinvar" to me. Here. I'm going to kiss you again.'

'That was a long one, wasn't it, Lynn? I forgot where I was. I forgot everything but you.'

'Forget me as well, love.'

'Lynn, what do you mean?'

'Goodbye, Prof, love.'

'Lynn! What's the matter?'

'God bless.'

'Lynn! Where are you going? Lynn. Lynn.'

A dark blue car stopped in the parking space. Mr Hollis stepped out. He put an arm through Graham's. Sam Bell appeared out of the shadows and stood at the boy's other side.

'Come on,' said Mr Hollis. 'It's all over.'

14

'Graham,' said his father.

'Yes.'

'You won't do anything silly, will you? Like opening the car door and jumping out?'

'No.'

'Promise me.'

'I won't do anything like that.'

'Good. I'm glad you have some sense. We'll be home in about three hours, with luck. Your mother has been ill with worry. But she has agreed not to talk about it. You can tell us everything when you are ready.'

'There's nothing to tell. And there never will be. You said yourself, it's all over. Isn't that enough?'

'Graham.'

'Yes.'

'Were you asleep?'

'No.'

'I had a word with the girl. While you were waiting with Mr Bell.'

'Waiting with Mr Bell,' Graham gave a little laugh. 'That's your story! Mr Bell was holding my arm . . . hard.'

'I'm sorry, Graham. But he couldn't let you go. Anyway, I had a word with the girl, Lynn. She told me that nothing happened.'

'What do you mean?'

'You know what I mean. You know very well what I mean. Now, Graham, I don't really believe it myself. You're a young man. You didn't do all this just to look into her beautiful blue eyes. But that's what she says. And that's what I shall tell your mother.'

'You can tell her what you like.'

'Listen, Graham. I don't care if it's true or not. It's what I want your mother to believe. And I don't want you to tell her anything else.'

'Why not?'

'Because it'll hurt her. You've hurt her enough.'

'She hid the valuables while Lynn was watching.'

'Forget that now. We must all agree not to mention it again. Right?'

'I suppose so.'

'In a way we're all very lucky. We told people that you were staying with your grandmother. Nobody knows what has happened. So remember where you have been. On a visit to your grandmother. Right?'

'All right. If that's what you say.'

'Graham.'

'Yes.'

'Come on, son. It's not the end of the world.'

'It is for me.'

'Rubbish. You'll forget all about it. It was important for a while. And now it's finished. It's ended happily, with nobody worse off. But it *did* cost me a little money.'

'What do you mean?'

'We planned to meet you at that parking space. I didn't just happen to be passing. Perhaps you want to know how it was done?'

'No, I don't.'

'I think you should, Graham. I'll tell you the whole story.'

'I don't want to hear it.'

'We were still looking for you, without success, at lunch time today. And then I had a telephone call from Mr Wright, the owner of Jeff's Café. He told me that he knew where you were. The Royal Britannia Hotel in Cobchester.'

'I'm not listening. I tell you I'm not listening.'

'You see, Lynn phoned and told him everything. But we didn't think the girl could keep you at the hotel. Anyway, we didn't want to make trouble *there*. Are you listening *now*, Graham?'

'No.'

'Mr Wright knew this man Bell who will do almost anything for a few pounds. We planned to meet you at that parking space. The first one past the crossroads with the Crimley road. It cost me seventy pounds, Graham.'

'I didn't ask you to pay it.'

'I know you didn't. But I paid it all the same. Twenty pounds for Mr Bell.'

'How nice for him. And fifty for Jeff, I suppose.'

'Oh no, Graham. Nothing for Mr Wright. He just wanted his girl back. The fifty was for her.'

'What? She took money from you?'

'She certainly did. That's what I wanted you to know. She took the money and she told me to tell you. She wanted you to know about the money. That's how much she cared for your feelings.'

'I don't believe you.'

'It's true. She sold you, Graham. She sold you for fifty pounds. Fifty pounds in five pound notes.'

—She's a cow.

—Shut up.

—A dirty little cow. She belongs on the streets.

—Shut up.

—A two-faced dirty little cow.

—No. Not Lynn. No.

—Do you think your father was telling the truth?

—No.

—Do you think your father was telling the truth?

—No. No.

—Do you think your father was telling the truth?

—Yes. Oh Lynn, you couldn't, you didn't. I love you.

—You *did* love her. You don't now.

—I do.

—She sold you. For fifty pounds.

88

—She said she loved me. She was kind to me. Again and again.

—Fifty pounds.

—Shut up.

—No arguing with facts.

—Love's not about facts. Love's about people. I don't understand, but I love her. She's good, I know she's good.

—Fifty pounds.

—I'll love her till I die.

—You don't love her. You only thought you did. It wasn't real. You'll soon forget her. She sold you. You won't forget that. She sold you for fifty pounds.

15

'Is it nice, Graham?'

'Yes, mother.'

'Better than those school dinners?'

'Yes, mother.'

'I feel sorry for the boys who can't get home at midday. I do think boys need a good midday dinner when they're growing.'

'Yes, mother.'

'I must say you're looking quite well these days. I worried about you after *it* happened. You were so white and ill. Oh, Graham, how *could* you . . .?'

'Mother!'

'I know we don't talk about it. Well, you don't talk about it to *me*. I sometimes think your father knows more than I do. Oh, yes, I nearly forgot. He rang this morning. He wants you to go and see him this afternoon after school.'

'What does he mean? I see him every day.'

'He meant at the office. He wants you to call at the office.'

'I wonder why. Did he sound angry?'

'No, not at all. He wants to talk to you about something. He thought the office was the right place.'

'Your father will see you now, Mr Graham.' Graham closed the office door behind him.

'He called me "Mr Graham", Father. Old Benson called me "Mr Graham".'

'Yes, do you mind?'

'No. It sounded odd, that's all.'

'It's old-fashioned. But then Benson is old-fashioned. He's been here for seventeen years, you know.'

'It's all the same to me. I don't care what people call me.'

'It means something to him. This is a family business, Graham. The people who work for us are part of a family. They've been with me a long time. I value them, and one day you'll value them too. When you take over the company. But I'm not thinking of leaving for a long time yet.'

'I didn't think you were,' Graham said drily.

'Don't speak to me like that!' said Mr Hollis.

'Sorry, Father.'

'All right, son, forget it. I suppose you were wondering why I asked you to come here.'

'Yes.'

'Well, I wanted you to get to know us all better. But I've also got something I want to tell you. It's to do with your little adventure a few weeks ago.'

'I don't want to talk about it.'

'Neither do I, Graham. And I very nearly decided not to. I got something through the post last week. I didn't know if I should show it to you. But after careful thought I felt that I must. Take a look at this, will you? An envelope addressed to me with a London postmark. And inside it, fifty pounds. No letter, nothing else at all, just fifty pounds. I thought this might shake you, and it has. You know who it is from, of course?'

'Yes.'

'It's interesting. It's the same fifty pounds that I gave her. I took the numbers of the notes. It's a little habit of mine. I always do it when I am paying for something unusual. These are the ten five-pound notes that I handed to your friend Lynn, when we were up there on the road to Scotland. Now, Graham, do you know anything about it?'

'No.'

'You haven't heard from her?'

'No.'

'Never? In any shape or form?'

'No.'

'I've been thinking about it all week and I still don't understand. But I felt I ought to tell you. I couldn't *not* tell you. I had to be fair to the girl.'

'So she didn't sell me,' Graham said slowly. 'She didn't sell me. She gave me back.'

'Well, yes, I suppose she did.'

'I should have known. She never meant to keep your money. When you tried to give her money before, she refused it. She said you didn't have to pay her to go away. She didn't care about money. But why did she take it, then? Why *hand* me back to you? Why?'

'I don't know, Graham, but I'm glad she returned it. The fifty pounds doesn't matter. It's good to know that a girl like that is not completely bad.'

'Not completely bad? You make me sick. You don't have any right to say things like that about Lynn. She's better than a hundred of us.'

'I hope you're not going to do anything silly, Graham. You were beginning to get back to everyday life. Perhaps I shouldn't have told you.'

'Why did she do it? That's what I want to know. If only I could find her, and ask!'

'You won't find her now. And anyway, Graham, I think the moment has passed.'

'We'll see about that.'

'Alice!'

'What? Who is it?'

'Alice. It's me, Graham. You remember me?'

'Yes, I remember you.'

'Where's Jeff?'

'Out.'

'Will he be long?'

'What's it to do with you?'

'I wanted a word with you, that's all.'

'With *me*? All right, come round the back. Here, have a cup of tea, it's fresh. Jeff's just gone across the road. He'll be away for about half an hour. Well, what do you want?'

'Alice, where's Lynn?'

'How should I know?'

'She's left?'

'Yes.'

'You haven't heard from her?'

'No.'

'When did she leave?'

'You ought to know that. She left the day that you did.'

'What? You mean she hasn't been back?'

'No. I haven't seen her.'

'But what about Jeff?'

'Jeff's all right. We've got a new girl in the café now. Sally. Long black hair. Jeff likes her better than he liked Lynn. He's not worrying.'

'But . . . I thought Jeff went to get her back. From the road to Scotland.'

'Oh yes. So he did. Well, he *meant* to bring her back. But before he arrived, Lynn crossed the road and hitched a ride going the other way. When he got there she wasn't waiting for him. Jeff was angry with Sam Bell. But, as Sam said, there was nothing he could do about it. Sam never cared much for Jeff anyway.'

'So you don't know where Lynn is now?'

'I told you. No.'

'My father has a letter which we think is from her. Post-marked London.'

'Then that's where she is. And doing no good either if I know Lynn. Still, I've known worse. – the girl we've got now. The way Sally manages to get what she wants, it's hard to believe. Why, only the other day . . .'

'Thanks for the tea, Alice.'

'That's all right. Drop in any time you want. Jeff won't mind. Don't be afraid of him. He's forgotten Lynn already.'

'Do you think you'll ever hear from her, Alice?'

'No, of course not. When a girl like Lynn leaves a place like this, she leaves it for ever. She's gone like many before her. Into thin air.'

—Think. Be the accountant's son. Look at the facts. Find an

answer. Quietly. And don't try to fool yourself. It started by accident. She was finished with Jeff. She went off with you. As a joke, almost. But when she stopped to think, what then? What did you have to offer? Not much. A cheap flat somewhere, jobs for both of you. In three or four years' time, children. And never free again. Oh, yes, you wanted to marry her. Fine. But why should she want to marry you?

—Come on. Think it out. That's not all.

—No, that's not all. You know you weren't a great catch for her. But she could have just walked out. Why did she give you away? Why did she cry? Why take fifty pounds like a woman of the streets, and then send it back?

—Well, go on. Why?

—For your own good, you fool. That's why. She knew what was best for you. There was only one way to make you go home and stay there. That's why she took the money. She wanted you to think badly of her. The only way to stop you pulling the world down around your parents' ears.

—She loved you, she said so. She loved you enough to leave you. She kept the money till you were safely back in your old life. Till it was too late. Because it *is* too late, isn't it?

—She thought I was weak, didn't she? She thought I wasn't brave enough to be free. Maybe she was right. Or maybe she knew it wasn't my kind of freedom. Oh, Lynn, you knew too much. But nothing's the same now, not even Hollis and Son. In nine days you changed everything. And you did love me, didn't you, Lynn? More than you ever loved anyone. Even Butch.

. . . He was walking on cliffs, somewhere on the South Coast. Somewhere quiet and beautiful. White chalky cliffs where the green hills came to a stop. It was a clear blue day. He could hear sea-birds calling. She came to him along the cliff-top.

'Prof!' she called to him.

'Lynn!' he called back. 'Lynn it's you at last. Lynn! Lynn! . . .'

—Come off it boy. Put away childish things. Don't be a fool. She's gone, like many before her. Gone into thin air. Gone.

—I might see her again sometime.

—You won't.

—I'll never marry anyone else.

94

—You will.

—All right, it's over now. The end of the day. Tomorrow is another. Take it easy, don't *worry* so. Goodnight, Prof, love. Goodnight, Lynn, love. God bless.

Glossary

(The glossary gives the meaning of the word as it is used in this book. Other possible meanings are not given.)

accountant a man who manages money matters for companies, businesses, and rich people

Casanova an Italian who became famous as a great lover of women (d. 1798)

cliff a high rock face, often at the edge of the sea

counter a table in a shop behind which the shopkeeper stands

customer a person who buys things

fish and chips *fried* fish and *fried* potatoes, often sold in 'fish and chip' shops (see *to fry*)

fry to cook in oil or fat

hitch-hike to get a free ride by asking for one (from the driver of a car, lorry, etc.)

hot-dog hot sausage in bread – often sold on the street

jealous to feel angry because someone else has something you want. A man is sometimes *jealous* if his wife dances with another man

juke-box automatic record-player in cafés and bars – it is worked by coins

porter a man who carries cases at railway stations, hotels, etc.

silly not clever, not important

smoke *smoke* rises from a fire. *Smoke* comes from a cigarette when it is alight. When you breathe in *smoke* from a cigarette, you are *smoking*

spot a small mark on something; a place